The Life and Times
of a Country Peddler

D1457982

FIRST EDITION

Copyright © 1999 by Ira G. Carter

Published by Vantage Press, Inc.
516 West 34th Street, New York, New York 10001

Manufactured in the United States of America
ISBN: 0-533-13070-0

Library of Congress Catalog Card No.: 99-93574

0 9 8 7 6 5 4 3

The Life and Times of a Country Peddler

Ira G. Carter

VANTAGE PRESS
New York

To my wife, Hazel, who for 48 years has "scotched" for me
when I "pushed"

Contents

Introduction

Between 1950 and 1983 I worked as a sales representative and district trainer for a large corporation in the rural South. During these 33 1/2 years I heard some great stories and witnessed even more. This book is a compilation of some of those stories, most of which are basically true. Some are obviously laced with fiction. All are somewhat embellished. Most are of a humorous nature. Some few are in a more serious vein.

It is my belief that it is important that my grandchildren, their children and their children's children maintain some ties to the past. Even though they do not like to be reminded of "how it used to be," the record should be there for them. Hopefully this book will in some small way bridge the past to the present for these later generations.

My thanks go to good friend, Charles Harmond, general manager of the local newspaper, the *Commercial Dispatch*, Columbus, Mississippi, and to my friend and pastor, Dr. Bobby Douglas, pastor of First Baptist Church in Columbus, who encouraged me to make this compilation.

Thanks also go to a special friend, Donna Young, who labored tirelessly in helping me to put it all together.

Part I
Stories Basically True

The Lady and the Dog

After having called on a customer in Okolona, Mississippi, I walked out the front door of his place of business and headed down the sidewalk to my car which was parked some seventy-five feet down the street. Directly in front of me, and walking in the same direction as I, was a lovely, well-dressed lady. She was tall and willowy, with all the parts of the anatomy properly fitted together. Her hair was done up in a little ball on the side of her head, revealing a long, slender neck, and as she strolled along in front of me she literally rippled from the top of her head to her heels. She was truly a good looker—both coming and going.

But this is a story about a beautiful little dog, not about a woman. This fluffy little dog with slightly pointed ears, newly bathed and brushed, suddenly appeared on the sidewalk—in front of me and behind the lovely lady. Being a dog lover, my attention was immediately focused on the dog and the lovely lady was history.

Without thinking, I spoke to the little dog. "Come here, you pretty little thing, and let me pet you."

Not until the lady had slowed her pace and started to turn her head around and peer at me over her right shoulder did I realize she did not know the dog was there. To make matters worse, by the time the lady had turned to look, the dog had jumped off the sidewalk, down on the street and was resting under a parked car. Needless to say, I did the only thing any right thinking man would do under the circumstances. I dropped my little briefcase on the street, descended to my knees in all the grease and grime and pleaded with that little dog to please come out, all to no avail.

So far as I know that little dog is still under the car. And so far as I know, that lovely lady *still* doesn't know the little dog was a part of the scene.

Lose Some—Win Some

Whoever said "man's best laid plans so often go awry" must have been a salesman. I had planned a day's work for the next day. On paper, it looked perfect. I had a fistful of good promotions and an area of volume accounts to present them to. All these customers I was to see had in the past been receptive to this type promotion and had bought heavily. My last call of the day was to be a small wholesaler who serviced the area. His money was limited and a carload of soap products would cost a bundle, but I felt sure when I handed him a batch of orders for him to deliver that he would give me a carload order to close out the day. The adrenaline was flowing. I couldn't wait to get started.

After getting up early and eating a "lumberjack" breakfast, I piled into my car to begin the day. But the car wouldn't crank, and by the time a new battery was installed, I had lost an hour. The first customer I called on was in the process of selling his business to his son-in-law and wasn't interested in what I had to say. The next customer that I was counting on was, for the first time ever, gone to Augusta to see the "Big One" in golf. One disappointment after another all day.

Finally it was time to see my wholesaler and close out the day with a carload order. I parked out front and started up the steps into his office. My heart sank at what I saw. My primary competitor was just leaving and greeted me as though I was a long-lost friend. He was smiling victoriously from ear to ear. No way this little wholesaler was going to buy two carloads of soap products in one day, and he had obviously just bought one from my competitor.

It was getting dark by the time I checked in to the old hotel. I lugged my bags up the stairs and opened the door to my room. It was dark inside and as I felt around for a light switch I noticed a tiny beam of light coming through a tiny hole in the old wooden door that connected to the adjoining room. Suddenly the little beam of light went dark and I figured some "peeping Tom" had his eyeball pressed close to it.

Without turning on the light, I tiptoed lightly into the bathroom, out of his sight, and hummed softly in my best tenor voice as I turned on the light in the bathroom. I had been bothered with a sinus problem for several days and had in my possession the popular treatment in those days—a little bottle of powerful nasal spray. With the bottle came a pointed syringe with a rubber cap on the top. When the point of the syringe was put in the bottle and the rubber cap was pressed and then released, the syringe was filled. You would then hold your head back, push the point of the syringe up into your nose and press the rubber cap, squirting the medicine up into the sinus cavities. I quietly and quickly filled the syringe, slid down the wall out of sight of the "peeper," stuck the point of the loaded syringe in that tiny hole in the door and pressed the rubber cap. You would have thought someone had turned a wild bull loose in that room. Tables and chairs turned over and what sounded like a table lamp hit the floor. I quickly hung a coat on the door covering the peephole and washed up before going down to eat.

Out of curiosity I lingered in the lobby for a while, watching the people coming down the stairs. Shortly a pudgy, bald-headed, middle-aged man came waddling down the stairs. He looked as though he was about to bleed to death through his right eye as he mopped it. No question about it, he was old "Red-Eye."

The Chicken Mites

Many years ago the banking industry was much more fragmented than it is today. Every little town had its own privately owned bank. The local banker was looked upon as a near God-like figure, a guru, by the businessmen and residents in the surrounding area. He was always available to listen to problems of the locals. They could go to him and get advice on any matter. He would even loan them money if they had collateral with a value at least five times the amount of the loan they were seeking. The community's relationship with their banker was a very special one.

As the years passed, the larger banks in the larger towns began to buy these small town banks and change their names. This was a change the locals did not take lightly. As they saw it, they did not have a bank anymore. It now belonged to the big city slickers and the special relationship they had with their banker was no more. The local manager was usually left to run the bank, but now he had added responsibility. He had to convince the local businessmen and residents that nothing had really changed, that their relationship with the bank would be the same. In some cases this turned out to be a tough selling job.

One day I was calling on a customer in a small town where this had happened to their bank. My customer and I were in his office when the local banker came in to visit. It was obvious he was on a mission to soothe the nerves of my customer who was quite upset with the change in ownership of the bank. I was impressed with his brand of salesmanship—after all, he was trying to sell an intangible. His approach was entirely correct. He was light-hearted, confident and had a story to tell that grabbed my attention as well as my customer's.

As the story went, an elderly black couple had come to him to get a cash loan. The old man explained to the banker that they had lived for many years out in the northeast end of the county. Several years earlier electricity had become available to them and just a year ago a pump had been installed in their well and they now had running water in their house. Their next project was to put a bathroom in the house as some of their neighbors had done, but they would need a loan if they were to do it. The banker didn't know this old couple, so at this point he excused himself and went back into the bank to see if any employee knew them. Nobody knew them and their name was nowhere to be found in the bank records.

The banker returned to his office, took his seat behind his desk and asked the obvious question. "Mr. Brown, where have you been doing your business?"

The old man looked down at the floor and rather sheepishly answered, "We have been doing our business in the chicken house, but the chicken mites got so bad..."

Mr. "Shack" and His Dentures

The wholesale grocery business in rural areas has always been a tough and competitive business. To operate one successfully a manager had to be equally tough and competitive. Such was the case with Mr. J.D. "Shack" Shackelford of Louisville, Mississippi. Not only did he manage the business, but he also was the buyer of all carload merchandise. He was the man that I had to tangle with when it was, in my opinion, time for him to place an order for another carload of soap products. Of course he always thought I was trying to sell him too soon, and I always thought he was putting off buying too long. Hence the prolonged and sometimes loud discussions emanating from his office at times when I called on him.

Mr. "Shack's" office was situated in the corner of the building with windows down two sides, slightly overlooking the street outside. He positioned his desk in the corner so as to make it impossible for anyone to move around behind the desk with him. He demanded that salesmen sit directly across the desk from him during a sales presentation so he could "eyeball" them, as he put it. This made me uncomfortable at first. I always seemed to be more effective talking *with* a buyer rather than *at* him. However, I eventually became accustomed to his "eyeballing" me with those piercing eyes, hard set under bushy eyebrows.

On this particular call I was trying to sell him a carload of merchandise that I was convinced he needed to order for immediate delivery. (It was near the end of the month and I was behind quota on shipments for that month.) He was equally convinced that I was nuts to think he was ready to order. The dialogue grew louder as I continued to press him, giving all the reasons why he should order today. He countered with all the reasons why he was not going to buy.

I had noticed that he kept a glass of water on the corner of his desk, but on that call I was to learn that it was not for drinking. When he figured he had had enough of my persistence, he reached in his mouth, removed his false teeth and dropped them in that glass of water, making sure they were looking at me. I didn't even know he had false teeth!

At this point he had derailed my train of thought somewhat, but I decided to give him one more reason to buy. That's when he delivered the body punch. With his stubby fist he pounded the top of that old metal desk, setting up a vibration that rippled across the top of that desk to that glass of water and set those teeth to chattering at me. That did it, that blew my mind. I gathered my paper and left. Exiting the building, I got into my car and glanced up at his office. There stood Mr. "Shack," chest thrown out, arms crossed; he gave me a little wave as he smiled victoriously.

It was to be many years later when I visited him on his deathbed that I realized that not only did I respect this man for his honesty and business acumen . . . I loved him.

Bird Too Smart

A vital part of any salesman's job in a territory is proper planning. At the beginning of the year he will most likely be given a quota to ship during the year ahead. The salesman will then make his own monthly shipment plans at the beginning of each month. Production people take the total estimated sales plans from all the salesmen and schedule production accordingly. The factory wheels must be kept turning. Also important is the salesman's daily planning. He should list every call he expects to make that day, noting objectives to strive for, special situations likely to crop up, and any potential problems. I discovered early on that if a problem call is put off until the end of the day, concerns about it could hamper efficiency throughout the day. Problem situations should be handled as early in the day as possible. I always tried to plan the most pleasant call of the day for last. Ending the day on a pleasant note made for a more enjoyable night meal and a better night's sleep.

On this particular day I had planned my last call to be Mack's Grocery, a small store owned and operated by a delightful couple, Mack and his wife, Ellie. Ellie stayed around the front of the store, ran the cash register, and did what little buying was necessary. Mack, with some part-time help, handled the other responsibilities. Mack had a speech impairment; he stuttered terribly. If he became the least bit excited he simply could not communicate. Hence, he would let Ellie do most of the talking.

I walked into the store just before closing time to find Ellie and Mack alone in the store. Ellie was bent over the cash register laughing uncontrollably. From the back of the store I could hear Mack ranting, raving, and stutter-

10

ing. Up front we could hear him clearly as he yelled, "I'm a g-g-going to w-w-wring your d-d-darned n-n-neck!" Sandwiched in between Mack's rantings was the sound of a squawking bird.

Ellie eventually regained her composure sufficiently to explain to me what was going on. One of their children had given them a mynah bird to keep in the store, to, as they put it, "cheer things up around here." Mack promptly named the bird "Cato" and hung his cage back behind the meat market. The bird proved to be very intelligent and quickly learned to mock the conversation he heard in the store. Unfortunately for the bird, that was his downfall. The thing that threw Mack into such a rage was that "Cato" had learned to stutter.

Blackbird Pie

A change in the layout of my territory had made it necessary for me to spend one night each month in this small town that I had never spent the night in before. There were no motels in small rural towns at this time—only very old and very small hotels. On my arrival into town that morning I stopped by the desk in the old hotel and reserved my room before finishing the day's work. It was a cold and blustery February day and I was anxious at the end of the day to check into a warm hotel room. I lugged my bags up the creaky stairs and went down the hall to room "3." With my long-necked key I finally succeeded in unlocking the door to the coldest hotel room I had ever been in. The heating system consisted of a fireplace with a coal grate in it, a coal scuttle full of coal, some kindling wood, and a box of matches. I promptly pulled off my shoes and crawled into that bed with my clothes on. Next morning, there was a frost on the covers where my breath had frozen. One night was enough.

On my next trip into town I had learned that an elderly couple, Mr. and Mrs. Hull, lived in a large, two-story home just off the square and were taking in boarders. Their children were grown and gone. They enjoyed the company and I enjoyed access to their big country kitchen. Their house was always warm and smelled of food being cooked in that big kitchen. Mrs. Hull, a sweet and grandmotherly lady, must have spent half of her time there. I never saw her when she wasn't wearing both a smile and an apron. Mr. Hull was a hard-of-hearing, bumbling old geezer who seemed to always be in her way. He nevertheless had a certain glint in his eyes and a wry smile that made you wonder if maybe he knew something that you didn't know.

One afternoon I checked into the Hull home and there was a light carpet of snow on the ground. Mr. Hull approached me right away and asked me if I would go down to the barn with him. I agreed, of course, and he reached behind a door, picked up a 12-gauge long tom shotgun, got a handful of shells out of a cabinet and we walked down to his old barn. On the way down to the barn he confessed that he was craving a blackbird pie and he was sure I could help him get one. When I saw that flock of blackbirds around that barn I knew what he meant. We flushed the birds out and entered a stable at the end of the barn, and I awaited his instructions.

He loaded that long tom, handed it to me, told me to stick it through a crack in the back of the barn and shoot into the snow about one hundred feet away. I blasted away into that snow and the shot pattern was clearly visible. Mr. Hull took a hoe and cleaned the snow out of the area of the shot pattern. He then took a bucket of corn chops and spread it over the cleaned off area. We went back to the barn, reloaded that shotgun, stuck the barrel through that same crack and waited. Sure enough in about twenty minutes that flock of blackbirds came back in and covered the area he had baited with corn chops. I took careful aim and fired that blunderbuss into the concentration of blackbirds. Feathers flew and the area of that shot pattern was literally covered with dead birds, belly up. Mr. Hull let out a war whoop, took a feed basket and gathered thirty-seven dead blackbirds.

Sure enough, he dressed those birds and his sweet wife made his blackbird pie. Surprisingly it tasted a bit like chicken and dumplings. Not bad if you closed your eyes while trying to eat it.

The Reverend

During my thirty-three and one-half years working with the grocery industry in rural Mississippi, at both the wholesale and retail level, I came to know some wonderful people. "Preacher" was one such man. As I reflect on it now, I never knew his real name. He really was a preacher, a pastor of two small black churches. Based on my relationship with him in the warehouse, I would guess him to be a warm and caring pastor. He took much pride in getting to know each company representative that came through the warehouse, not by name but by the name of the company he represented. In my case, I was "Mr. Procter & Gamble."

Preacher had two severe physical impairments—his eyes were crossed and he had a cleft palate. In order for him to recognize a salesman he would have to move in closer, just about two feet away. Upon recognizing a salesman he would proudly and loudly proclaim the name of the company he worked for. Because of his cleft palate he had difficulty pronouncing the "C" and "K" sounds. They always came out as "P" sounds. In my case he would move in close, pucker his lips and say "Mr. Propter & Gamble." The trouble was that when he pronounced the "P" sound (twice in my case) he would literally spray you down with a shower of saliva. In the jargon of the pool room, he would spit in your face. After the third drenching, I figured a way to handle him without being offensive to him. I would watch him carefully as he moved in close. Then just as he puckered his lips I would quickly bend down to tie my shoe. As he delivered a hearty "Mr. Propter and Gamble" he would also deliver a saliva shower out into space where my face had been a second before.

"Dumbo" the Elephant

During my long tenure with the company that I worked for I spent some time as district trainer. That meant simply that I would go into a newly hired salesman's territory and work with him for several days, familiarizing him with the basics. One thing a new man must understand is that problems are always out there, that adversity will most certainly rear its ugly head now and then. The important thing is that we don't let adversity blow our minds. Rather, we face it head on, all the while trying to work ourselves around it, or through it, on our way to reaching the objective. Better still, take what appears to be adversity, turn it around and use it to your advantage. As an example of how this can be done, I used to tell the following story to the new salesmen.

This small circus operated in the southeastern part of the country, making its winter run in the southernmost areas and swinging up through the Carolinas, Georgia, Tennessee, and Alabama in the summer. An important part of the circus was Dumbo, a highly trained elephant that had been with the circus for many years. However, Dumbo was getting old, and suddenly one day he became stubborn to the point that he would not respond to any commands that trained elephants normally respond to. All he would do was stand tethered and eat five bales of hay every day. Adversity had struck.

The first order of business at that night's board meeting concerned Dumbo and what to do with him. He was a dead expense and was not producing, so it was agreed upon by all but one that Dumbo must be done away with. This one board member suggested that the circus use Dumbo's stubbornness to help them make money. His idea was to charge sporting-minded patrons a dollar each to make Dumbo sit down. If they were successful they could collect one hundred dollars. The other board members agreed to this since nobody had been able to make Dumbo do anything lately.

When the circus opened that night, Dumbo was tethered near a hawker who was shouting, "Step right up, ladies and gentlemen, pay a dollar, make the elephant sit down and take home one hundred dollars!" People began to fall in line and pay their dollars for a chance to make Dumbo sit down, hoping to win one hundred dollars. After all, making a highly trained elephant sit down shouldn't be too difficult. However, nothing worked. Dumbo just stood stubbornly, responding to nothing. Adversity had struck indeed, but had been faced head-on, had been turned around and was now being used to make money.

One warm spring night the circus was making a stand in a small town in the hills of north Georgia. "Step right up, ladies and gentlemen, pay a dollar, make the elephant sit down and take home one hundred dollars!" the hawker shouted. As usual, people fell in line with dollar bill in hand, waiting their turn. All of a sudden an old mountain man appeared on the edge of the crowd, leaning on his highly polished hickory walking stick. His broad-brimmed felt hat, greasy with many years' accumulation of perspiration, had little diamond shaped holes all around for ventilation. One gallus of his overalls was tied up with a string and the legs were too long, piling up on top of his brogan shoes. His long white beard was stained with tobacco juice that trailed down from each side of his mouth. Despite his personal appearance, lack of perception of what was going on was not a weakness of this old mountain man. Many a politician has learned too late that mountain men are, in fact, keenly perceptive.

After assessing the situation, the old man fell in line. He reached deep into his overalls pocket, pulled out a frayed Country Gentleman tobacco sack, loosened the draw-string and stripped out a moldy dollar bill. After tightening the draw-string and stuffing the tobacco sack back into his pocket, he hobbled up beside old Dumbo, patted his side affectionately and hobbled on around behind him. Then quick as a wink, and with all the strength he could muster, he clouted Dumbo's privates with that hickory walking stick. Dumbo threw his massive head into the air, bellowed loudly and sat down in the Georgia dust. The secret was out, everyone now knew how to make even a stubborn elephant sit down. Adversity had struck again.

At a called meeting of the board that night, a motion to finally dispose of Dumbo carried with one dissenting vote. This same board member again refused to let adversity blow his mind. His suggestion was to simply change the rules a bit. Instead of requiring that the elephant sit down, the successful bettor would have to make him shake his trunk up and down and from side to side. Again, this shouldn't be too difficult when working with a trained elephant. The board members agreed to give it a try and it worked well enough that Dumbo was kept on the team.

The circus made its winter swing south, moving up the coast in the spring and one year later was making a stand in that same little north Georgia town where Dumbo had encountered the old mountain man. But this year, remember, the rules were changed.

"Step right up, ladies and gentlemen, pay a dollar, make the elephant shake his trunk up and down and from side to side and take home one hundred dollars!" shouted the hawker.

Business was good, the crowd gathered, and suddenly out on the perimeter of the crowd appeared the same old mountain man, leaning on the same hickory walking stick, wearing the same hat, overalls and shoes. He squinted and spat tobacco juice through his lush gray beard as he keenly surveyed the situation. He stripped another moldy dollar out of his sack and handed it to the hawker as the hawker again shouted, "...make the elephant shake his trunk up and down and from side to side and take home one hundred dollars!"

As the old man hobbled up alongside Dumbo, the old elephant suddenly stopped munching on that bale of hay, stood bolt upright, tilted his head to the right and watched every move the old man made. Old Dumbo might be stubborn but he was by no means dumb—had a good memory too.

Slowly the old man stepped in close, raised Dumbo's massive right ear and in a low voice said, "Elephant, do you remember me?"

Dumbo quickly shook his trunk up and down.

The old man continued, "Elephant, do you want me to clout you again across your privates with this hickory stick?" Dumbo just as quickly shook his trunk from side to side.

I'm sure there was another called meeting of the board that night but I don't know what happened. You see, I was getting along in years at this time and at this point in the story had to make an urgent trip to the bathroom. When I returned, the narrator had finished.

Little Boy and the Rattlesnake

One day as I pulled up on the parking lot of a customer in Aberdeen, I noticed a bread delivery truck parked on the perimeter of the lot. The back doors of the truck were open wide and a crowd of people had pressed in close, on tiptoes, peering around one another and over other people's shoulders, trying to get a glimpse of whatever was in the back of the truck. The crowd was mixed—men, women, young, old, black, white, all very interested in whatever was in the back of that bread truck. I could not imagine that many people being that interested in donuts, honey buns, rolls or loaf bread. My own curiosity was aroused sufficiently that I too joined the peering crowd, standing on tiptoes, straining to see what was in the back of that bread truck. The sight that greeted me was scary and riveting. In a huge pile on the floor of that truck bed was the biggest rattlesnake that I had ever seen. The snake had been run over repeatedly by the truck driver and was in the throes of death. However, it was still moving, slowly, coiling and uncoiling as dying snakes will do.

As aforementioned, the crowd viewing the spectacle was mixed. Standing up closest to the snake was a young black boy, paralyzed with fear but apparently unable to separate himself from the scene. He was wearing a long-sleeved shirt and baggy pants that were about two sizes too large. The muscles in the side of his face were twitching with fear. The seat of his baggy pants was quivering as was his whole body. Suddenly I was aware that an elderly black man on a walking stick was edging his way through the crowd. The old man was well known around town. As he walked the streets on his hickory walking stick he would have a friendly greeting for everyone and a funny story for anyone who would stand hitched long enough for him to tell it.

As the old man made his way through the crowd, it was obvious to those of us who knew him that he was up to something. He had a particular twinkle in his eyes and a half smile as he worked himself into a position behind the little boy who was so scared. Quick as a wink, the old man used his walking stick to firmly "goose" the little boy in his behind. The little boy let out a blood-curdling scream and jumped straight up, arms over his head and legs apart. On coming back to earth he made his way over that crowd, over a car that was parked between him and wherever he was going, across the street and the last we saw of him was when he cleared an eight-foot privacy fence, continuing to scream his way into the distance.

What Goes Around Comes Around

On a rainy Monday morning my next call was the Big Star Supermarket on College Street. The only available parking space was across the street from the store entrance, and down aways. I sat in my car for a while waiting for the rain to let up and casually glanced over toward the front of the store. Old fashioned canvas awnings stretched across the front of the store and down one side. Through the years the canvas had begun to bag down between the metal support, and water would accumulate in these bags in large quantities.

Standing on the corner under the awning, out of the rain, was a rather large black man. I noticed that he was continually glancing up and down the sidewalk and then overhead to a large pocket of water that had accumulated on the awning. My curiosity was aroused by his behavior—I guessed he had thoughts about reaching up over his head and flipping the water out of the pocket in the awning. Sure enough, when nobody was on the sidewalk but him he surrendered to the temptation that had been gripping him. He stood on tiptoes and raised both hands over his head to flip that water off the awning. As he did so, his pants dropped to the ground around his ankles revealing a large pair of boxer shorts with bright blue vertical stripes. The poor fellow quickly re-panted himself and disappeared into the rain. What a pity that I was the only witness.

The rain let up shortly and I went into the store. The manager was standing in the paper products aisle where some stock clerks were opening toilet tissue and stocking the shelves. Toilet tissue cartons are cube shaped and about three feet each way. When emptying those boxes, stockers will open them with a case-opener knife and then close the flap back on the empty box. They are the perfect height for an adult to use as a seat.

I couldn't wait any longer to tell the manager about the fellow losing his pants out front. As I laughingly related to the manager what had happened, I backed up to what I thought was a case of toilet tissue and started to sit down. However, it was an empty box that the clerk had closed the flap on. Already I had shifted my weight backwards and I knew I was a goner—I slid all the way down into that empty box with nothing but my feet sticking out, with my face between them. It took me some time to extricate myself from that box and I got no help at all from the manager. He was busy summoning all the employees over to watch. They all got a much bigger laugh out of me trying to get out of that box than I had gotten from watching that poor fellow lose his pants out front. What goes around comes around.

And Now to Eat

Salesmen from the entire area used to plan their itineraries so as to arrive at the Ackerman Hotel in Ackerman, Mississippi, in time to get a room and a seat in the dining room for the night meal. And what a meal it was—at least three meats to choose from, every fresh vegetable in season, hot biscuits or corn bread, and coffee or tea. We weren't concerned with health foods in those days—we just wanted to fill our bellies with food that tasted good going down. Those little pieces of fatback floating around in the vegetables were pure flavor. Long tables with chairs all around them were piled high with all those goodies. The trick was to get yourself a seat at the end of the table. Sitting anywhere else meant you would have to spend half your time passing grub back and forth.

Mr. and Mrs. Sallis, the owners, were ideally suited to the business. He was rotund and jocular, always with a story to tell. She was the perfect complement—lovely and personable.

After pigging out, we would drag ourselves into the lobby and flop into oversize chairs to await the tale telling. It was always hard for me to pull away and go up to bed when these fellows were spinning yarns. Some of the stories, of course, were laced with fiction, but others were true accounts.

My favorite story was told by an elderly insurance salesman who had been combing the county all day chasing down leads. He pulled up to a farmhouse, got out of his car and introduced himself to a lady sitting in a front porch rocker shelling butter beans. She invited him to join her in the other rocker. He had no more than gotten comfortable when he noticed a sight that broke him up with laughter. Among the chickens pecking around in the yard was a rooster with no feathers and wearing a perfectly tailored pair of overalls. The lady explained to the salesman that the rooster had gotten caught in a tornado that sucked all his feathers out, so she had made the overalls to protect him somewhat from the elements. He responded that he believed this to be the funniest thing he had ever seen. As she continued to shell butterbeans, she remarked that if he thought that was funny, he should see that rooster trying to hold an old hen down with one foot while he tried to unbuckle those galluses with the other!

The Grass Is Greener

Ernie Pender had done quite well for himself. A black youngster, many years earlier he had started working for ABC Supermarket carrying out groceries, sweeping up and doing odd jobs. With the passage of time, the owner began to notice that Ernie was an exceptional young man. He proved to be intelligent, honest and hardworking. He was consequently rewarded with more and more responsibility and was eventually made assistant manager and buyer. It was in this capacity that I got to know Ernie. Though he and I didn't always agree, calling on him was always a pleasure.

Ernie and I had at least one thing in common—we both loved to fish and tell about it. It is said that the Lord will forgive a fisherman for stretching the truth a bit. Ernie needed this margin of safety—he certainly pressed his luck with the Lord, from time to time. I learned early on that the only way to tell a fish tale bigger than Ernie's was to let him finish his tale first. Ernie could tell a fish tale with so much emotion and animation that when he finished, I would feel as though I myself had been on a successful fishing trip.

About this time many youngsters from the South, both black and white, were migrating to the big cities of the North to jobs with better pay than they could get at home. Some of Ernie's friends had gone to Chicago and were urging Ernie to come on up and join them. Ernie and his wife had no children, so he had nothing to hold him back. After agonizing for several months, Ernie decided to make the move. He worked out his notice, loaded up his car, and drove to Chicago. His friends had a small apartment already lined up for him on the city's South Side. Two days later Ernie had a job at a factory within walking distance of his apartment. Things were falling into place.

As a new employee, Ernie had to work the midnight shift. At the end of the first week he got his pay—cash money, in an envelope. He was feeling good with that fat envelope on his hip as he struck out to the apartment in the dead of night along the nearly deserted streets. Along the way he noticed a man lying prone in the gutter near the curb. Being a country boy from the South, Ernie felt the compulsion to do something to help this poor man. However his better judgment prevailed and he decided to ignore the situation—this was another world he was living in now.

After walking on by, Ernie glanced over his shoulder one last time. What he saw was indeed fearsome. That prone body had risen to a three-point stance and had kicked off in Ernie's direction. He apparently knew Ernie had been paid and had the cash on him. What that fellow didn't know was that when a country boy from Mississippi is sufficiently motivated by fear, he can run like a deer.

Ernie grabbed that pay envelope with his left hand, laid his ears back, pointed his head toward his apartment and started to "pick 'em up and put 'em down" in a way that the fellow chasing him had never seen. In no time at all, Ernie had put so much distance between them that the pursuer dropped out of the race.

Ernie was totally exhausted when he got to the apartment and fell across the bed. It was some time before he could explain to his wife what had happened.

Early the next morning Ernie and his wife were packed up and heading south out of Chicago on their way home to Mississippi. One week later he was back on his old job at ABC Supermarket making a little less money but enjoying life considerably more.

To Climb a Mountain

New salesmen in the large company that I worked for would be accompanied in their own territory by a "trainer," an experienced salesman, for a week or two. During this time the rookie would be introduced to basic sales procedures, company policy, proper handling of required reports and the products he was selling. When the trainer left, the territory became the responsibility of the new man. As the new man began to call on customers, with no back-up, the learning experience was to begin in earnest.

During my tenure as a trainer I saw various

responses from new men who suddenly had the mantle of responsibility placed around their necks. Some would very nearly panic with fear. Others would be cocky and confident. Those that were fearful would most likely develop into productive employees. Those that were cocky and confident would most likely be humbled the first week they were on their own. Part of my advice to new salesmen that I had trained was to remember that when visiting management people began to ask questions, they were already in possession of the answers.

As a new man with the company, my trainer had left me with the weight and responsibility of the territory and I was quaking in my boots under the load. The night before I had slept little, thinking about the next day's work schedule. I was to call on and sell a carload of soap to a man known far and wide as the meanest buyer south of the Mason-Dixon Line. The word was that he loved to have new salesmen call on him. He would literally "chew 'em up and spit 'em out."

I decided to park on a side street and enter the warehouse through the shipping department rather than run the risk of encountering "Mr. C" in the front office. As I checked my inventory back in the warehouse I could hear a booming voice that sounded like a foghorn barking out commands to workers. The acoustics in that warehouse were frightening. The sound of "Mr. C's" voice kept bouncing around among the rafters. My palms were so sweaty I could hardly hold a pencil. My knees were shaking but the time had come for me to face the monster. I could tell that "Mr. C" was pacing back and forth between the office and the shipping desk so I positioned myself alongside that walkway and waited.

Shortly I saw the office door crack open and heard

that voice again. Any moment now that giant of a man, that mean monster, would be in my face. To my astonishment, out of that office door stepped a diminutive character, not over five feet two inches tall and weighing no more than one hundred and ten pounds. He was ninety-five percent mouth. As is often the case with small men, all his clothes were too big. The shoulders of his shirt sagged down halfway to his elbows and his sleeves were rolled up just above his wrists. His oversized pants were gathered around his waist and the too-long legs were stacked up on top of his shoes, mopping the dust from the warehouse floor as he strutted back and forth. An oversized felt hat with the sides rolled up rested on the tops of his ears. I stood erect and tried in vain to appear confident as he approached me.

Surprisingly he stomped right on past me, almost stepping on my toes, never looking at me. Three times he passed me by as though I didn't exist and I was beginning to relax just a bit. Then on his fourth pass he stopped directly in front of me, turned toward me, stomped his foot and in a voice that could be heard all over that warehouse said "Boy, what the h— do you want?" In later years we were to laugh about how close he came to getting stepped on that morning since he was standing between me and the only way out of the place.

"Mr. C" had done what he set out to do—he had scared the daylights out of a new salesman. It was downhill for me from there on. We went to his office; he introduced me to the people there and sat down behind his desk, never bothering to remove that old felt hat. We worked up a carload order, he signed it and I left. I felt every bit of seven feet tall. My first day on my own and I had sold a carload order to the meanest buyer south of the

Mason-Dixon Line! Bring on Mt. Everest.

Old "Bo"—Killer Dog

The E.L. Bruce Company Store, Bruce, Mississippi, was a Wal-Mart type retail outlet long before Mr. Sam Walton ever had a store—that is, except for the prices. They sold everything from fatback to rocking chairs to cowboy boots to horse collars to aspirin tablets. Incidentally, the store sold soap powder also—by the truckload. Their volume necessitated the use of a large warehouse out back to hold reserve merchandise. The warehouse was located about seventy-five feet out behind the retail store building and was connected by a concrete walkway.

The location and layout of the warehouse made it a popular target for thieves. In fact, break-ins became so bad that it was decided to build a chain link fence around the warehouse, tying into each back corner of the store. Then another chain link fence was built running from the front of the warehouse, along the edge of the concrete walkway, tying into the back of the retail store. This created a small pen with access to the warehouse area by way of a heavy metal gate. The small pen was to keep a guard dog confined during the daytime when workers had to be moving back and forth from store to warehouse. At night the steel gate would be opened and the guard dog would be free to roam all around the warehouse.

In order to make this thing work it was necessary for the management to find a notoriously mean guard dog. In this endeavor they were indeed successful. Old "Bo" was without a doubt the biggest and meanest dog I had ever seen. He was big as a bear and had a head and tusks like one. Of course he was fastened in the small pen during the daytime while workers and salesmen were moving back and forth between store and warehouse. I have always loved dogs of all kinds but old "Bo" reacted violently to all my attempts to build a relationship with him. In fact, each time I walked along that fence on my way to the warehouse, he lunged at me every step of the way, snarling and slobbering through those long tusks. As I passed that heavy metal gate, I always checked to be sure it was fastened before I went into the warehouse.

One day, I walked into the store to find it overflowing with customers. All the employees were busy and the buyer, Rube Thomas, gave me no indication he even knew I was present. Rube, after you got to know him, was a first magnitude gentleman. He loved to "fun around" as he called it, but woe unto you if you were one of his victims. What he called "funning around" could be borderline torture to his victims. For instance, when young new sales reps came in for the first time, he would direct them out to the warehouse to check inventory of their merchandise. Once the young salesman was in the warehouse, Rube would recruit about three of his big tough buddies, go out to the warehouse, and while some of them held the young man, the others would pull down his pants and literally saturate his privates with price marker ink. Nothing would remove this kind of ink. It had to wear off, and that took a while. You be the judge—was Rube fun-loving or torturous?

Back to my experience on that day. Since Rube was so busy and since I had been calling on him for so long, I knew it was perfectly all right for me to go out to the warehouse and check my inventory without his permission. As I walked along that fence, an enraged Bo lunged at me continuously. I checked the metal gate just to be sure it was fastened before I went into the warehouse. Once inside the warehouse, one half of my mind was checking inventory and the other half was thinking about what would happen to me if old Bo were to somehow get out of that pen. He would have me cornered, and with those long tusks he would go for the jugular. My next fishing partner would be St. Peter.

About this time I heard Rube talking to old Bo. (Rube was the only one Bo would not attack: he fed Bo a piece of prime beef every day.) Rube did know I was in the warehouse and he was talking just loud enough for me to hear him. His words went something like this: "Come on Bo, there's nobody out there—come out here and stretch your legs." Filled with terror, I yelled at the top of my voice, "Rube, I'm in here—don't let that dog out!" Rube, pretending not to hear me, rattled that metal gate as though opening it, and again told Bo to stretch his legs. This warehouse had cross-timbers or ceiling joists about twelve feet off the floor and someone had stored an extra mattress on top of these joists. The next thing I remember is that I was flat on my belly on top of that mattress, my eyes on the front door, watching for that killer dog to come after me. However, what came in that door was something else entirely—the fun-loving Rube Thomas, looking for me. When he finally spotted me twelve feet up, flat on my belly and bug-eyed with fear, he laughed so hard and so long that he simply piled up on the floor. After eventually regaining his composure he found a ladder and helped me down. Neither of us could figure out how I got up there.

Shortly after this little bit of "funning around" by

Rube Thomas, he died suddenly. I miss you, Rube.

Say What?

A newcomer in the sales field or, for that matter, any other person desiring to be effective in people-to-people relationships, learns early on that what people are *saying* and what they are *thinking* are not always the same. All too often the spoken word is a façade. What's going on in the mind is something else entirely. If we are to deal with other people effectively we must develop the skills that will enable us to delve behind the façade and make an accurate determination of what he or she is thinking. In the final analysis we deal with what is going on in his or her mind. It is imperative that the salesman learn to deal with this if he is to be successful.

Mr. Harmond was the perfect gentleman—courteous, polite, soft-spoken and gentle. He was also the classic example of the person who was habitually saying one thing and thinking something else. As majority owner and carload buyer for a wholesale grocery company, he and I faced each other regularly across his desk. After many years of calling on him, a business relationship ripened into a warm personal one. I found myself calling on him in the afternoons after which he would lock the office and he and I would visit in his boat at a private lake that he had access to. No other setting is as conducive to the "getting to know each other" process.

During my first few calls on Mr. Harmond I would come away frustrated and ineffective. I simply could not read him. That, however, was to change on what I considered to be my first successful call on this good man. I got exactly what I wanted and he got what he wanted—the perfect call.

According to my calculations, it was time for him to place an order for a carload (ten tons) of soap products. I decided to do as I had been taught and give him a choice between "something and something" rather than a choice between "something and nothing." In other words, I was planning to check his inventory and ask him to do something he had never done before—buy *two* carloads to be shipped two weeks apart.

I was a bit nervous and somewhat excited as I walked through the front office, spoke to the people there and entered the warehouse for an inventory check. After planning out *two* carload orders I returned to the office awaiting my turn. Pride consumed me—I was thinking big. My gun was loaded and I was ready for the kill.

Mr. Harmond called me in and we exchanged the usual greetings. As we got down to business, I placed before him on his desk my carefully prepared plan for him to order the two carloads to be shipped two weeks apart. He studied my suggestion carefully and his brow furrowed deeply. Being the perfect gentleman, he didn't fire back emotionally at my ridiculous proposal. He simply launched into a familiar harangue about how slow business had been, how his top salesman was threatening to quit, how a plant in town was closing, etc., etc. All the time he is talking, I figure he is thinking something else entirely. He is thinking how a young "whippersnapper" like me must be crazy to think he would let me dictate to him how to run his business—how much to buy, and when to ship it.

At the conclusion of his little speech, in his soft-spoken manner he simply told me, "Young man, there is no way I could buy *two* carloads of your merchandise." Right away I knew I had sold the *one* carload I expected to get in the first place. Mr. Harmond felt good inside because he had gently but firmly let a young salesman know that he, himself, was running his business and making the decisions as to how much to buy and when to buy it. I was happy to get the carload order. A good day was had by all.

Jake and the Bear

Bad news is as contagious as the mumps. All over my territory industries were furloughing their employees. Consumers were stretching their dollars, buying less. Inventories were backing up in warehouses and some wholesalers were having trouble paying their bills. It seemed that everyone in business had caught the "blahs." A happy face was a rare sight. I was behind on quota, and that year-end bonus was indeed in jeopardy.

Mercifully July came around and it was time for my two weeks of vacation. What a godsend. An old college roommate who had gone to Chicago and made his fortune called and invited me to go on a Canadian wilderness fishing trip with him at his expense. All of a sudden things were looking up. There is simply nothing more enjoyable than spending a day fishing with a good friend whose company you enjoy.

I flew into Memphis where I was joined by "Jake," another old college buddy, and we flew into Chicago where we spent the night. From there we drove to Kenora, Ontario, a pleasant little town nestled on the shore of a lake that was studded with float planes carrying fishermen into the wilderness country. We took our gear down a narrow street to the water's edge and waited on a pier for our plane, an old British "Otter" float plane. Jake had never been able to overcome his fear of flying. As we waited on the pier Jake was bug-eyed, pasty-faced, white-knuckled and had to "wee wee." A local pointed up the little street where there was a public restroom and Jake went briskly in search. He spotted an open doorway leading into a hall. At the end of the hall he saw a commode. Jake walked through that open door, down that little hallway and into the restroom where he unzipped his pants and began to take care of business. Just as he zipped up his pants and turned to leave, he found the hall blocked by a Chinese man, his wife and four children. They were all jabbering, gesturing and screaming at him. Jake had unknowingly walked through the front door of a Chinese family's home and was helping himself to their bathroom.

We arrived at the fish camp late in the afternoon and all the talk was about a black bear that had been seen on the premises. If there was anything Jake was more afraid of than flying, it was bears. Jake and I shared a cabin and he talked about that bear until the wee hours before finally falling asleep.

The owner of the fish camp had a beautiful black Labrador retriever appropriately named "Midnight." Like most Labs, he was hung up on retrieving. He carried a stick in his mouth all the time begging someone to toss it so he could retrieve it. We would throw a stick off a ten-foot embankment into the lake and he would leap into the water spread-eagled to retrieve it.

Early the next morning there was a knock on our

door and a call to breakfast. I got up but couldn't get Jake to respond. After dreaming about huge killer bears all night, he was finally snoring loudly. I knew better than to try to shake him awake. If you tried to wake him by touching him he would deliver a devastating right hook with lightning speed and later swear that he remembered nothing about it. Suddenly I got an idea. Where was Midnight? I opened the cabin door and that dog came running up to me with a stick in his mouth begging me to throw it. Opportunities like this come around once in a lifetime. I opened the cabin door wide, took the stick from a begging Midnight and tossed it across Jake's bed and to the floor beyond. That huge black dog bounded onto Jake's bed and clambered over it in search of the stick. At the same time this was going on I yelled "Bear! Bear!" For the remainder of our stay at the fish camp Jake was the first one up every morning.

The Rotted Cheese

In the 1950s and early 1960s the retail grocery industry was so very different than today. There were no supermarkets, as we now know them. Small neighborhood stores were scattered throughout the residential areas, giving personal service to the ladies in the area. If the customer wanted a certain cut of meat, the butcher would dig a beef out of the cooler and cut it for her. If she needed help getting her groceries home, she could get it. If she needed credit, no problem with that. The more successful neighborhood grocer knew all about his customers. He would know the names of their cats and dogs, the names of all their kids, where they went to church, all their likes and dislikes.

Just such a grocer was Mr. Bob. His small shotgun store sat on a corner lot. He had one cash register up front, some produce down one side, some milk, cheese and eggs down the other side and two gondolas down the middle that held the other groceries. There was a small meat case across the back. You had to tell the butcher what you wanted and he would get it out of the case, wrap it in brown paper, weigh it and mark the price on it. A door in the back opened into a fenced area which doubled as a pen for "Old Rambler," his fortunate hound dog. Old Rambler must have been the best-fed dog in town. In fact, he had become so picky that he would eat only the best cuts of meat. If it was the least bit old or tainted he wouldn't touch it. All he did was eat and sleep. He lived the kind of dog's life that my dogs never dreamed of.

One morning Mrs. Andrews made her usual trip down to Mr. Bob's store to buy the day's groceries. On this particular day she was to buy an item she had never before purchased . . . Limburger cheese. She was not familiar with it, but had heard some of the other ladies discussing a recipe that called for it. After paying for her little sack of groceries she walked out the door and to her house up the street. After a few minutes Mr. Bob's phone rang. It was Mrs. Andrews, and she was livid at Mr. Bob for selling her some cheese that was rotten. Mr. Bob tried to explain to her that there was nothing wrong with the cheese, that all Limburger cheese smelled that way. Convincing her was not easy, so he told her to bring the cheese back to the store. He explained to her, on her return, that his old dog Rambler wouldn't touch any kind of food that was old, tainted, or rotten. Why not throw old

Rambler a piece of that Limburger cheese and if he would eat it, then Mr. Bob's point would be proved.

They walked to the back of the store, opened the door and Mr. Bob called to Rambler. That overweight old hound lazily came to his feet and walked over to Mr. Bob, at which point Mr. Bob tossed him a piece of the smelly cheese. Old Rambler gulped that cheese down, making Mr. Bob proud. "See, I told you that cheese was okay," he said to Mrs. Andrews. But Mr. Bob's pride was short lived. Old Rambler dragged himself slowly over into the shade of his fig bush, flopped down on his side, and as dogs will do sometimes, started licking his bottom. Mrs. Andrews was quick to add to the exchange taking place between them. "I told you that cheese was rotten, and it is. Already that dog is trying to get that bad taste out of his mouth."

A Car and Expenses

When interviewing for my job, I couldn't see past the offer of a "car and expenses furnished." Whatever downside the job might have, it would be more than offset by my getting a new car every year and being able to stay in motels and eat in restaurants without having to pay for it with my own money.

Being a child of the Depression, I never did learn to feel comfortable spending the kind of money we used to spend at sales meetings. Inevitably, when I would retire to my room at night during sales meetings, I would lie across my bed and reflect on how it used to be. How as a kid during the 1930s I never had any money. I would think about how I used to linger at the feet of my dad as he and his neighbors would stand around and talk. From my vantage point they all looked seven feet tall, and they always had their right hands stuck deep down into the right pocket of their overalls rattling their money. *Wouldn't it be great to have some money to rattle!* I would think to myself.

When I was about eight years old my Dad decided it was time for me to have a "piece of the pie." He gave me one whole row in the garden. Whatever I raised on it I could sell and have the money. I elected to go with radishes. Nothing in the garden was as pretty to me as a freshly washed bunch of radishes, all red and white and green and ready to eat.

From the day I planted my row of radishes until the day they were ready to harvest seemed an eternity to me. I would check on them every day, pluck out all the weeds and grass and stir up the soil around them just as Dad told me to do. They seemed to grow so very slowly. I remember one of my dad's favorite expressions was "a watched pot is slow to boil," and I for the first time came to understand what he meant.

Eventually my radish crop was ready for the harvest. Late in the afternoon I gathered enough to make six bunches, washed them thoroughly and loaded them into the back of our T-Model truck. Early next morning my dad let me ride into down with him to peddle our produce. I had never been happier. We drove into town and Dad parked in front of a grocery store. He told me I was on my own, to take the radishes in the store and see if I could sell them to the owner. Surprisingly the merchant agreed to buy all six bunches, for five cents per bunch. I took him up on his deal and he gave me two dimes, one nickel and five pennies which I promptly deposited deep down in the right front pocket of my overalls.

Next day my dad and a couple of his friends were standing in our yard talking and rattling their money as usual. I promptly joined them, standing at my dad's feet, looking up at them with my right hand stuck deep down into my right overalls pocket, rattling those two dimes, one nickel and five pennies.

And Now for Dessert

The day had been a long and particularly stressful one. After many miles of driving and after dealing with a very difficult customer, the sun was low in the afternoon sky and my motel was just over the next hill. What a welcome sight! I dragged myself into my room, went into the bathroom to wash my hands and face and to do the other things older men always do when they come across a bathroom, and then flopped across the bed. My eyes were heavy and my stomach was empty—I had to make a choice. Hunger won out and I walked over to the motel café. There were bigger and better restaurants in town but I was too tired to do any more driving.

As I walked into the restaurant, a petite and charming little waitress greeted me cheerfully, and escorted me to a table over in her section. Just being in the presence of this happy little lady made me feel somewhat rested already. Her smile seemed so natural, and she wore it so very well, as she bounced back and forth between kitchen and tables, pouring coffee and tea to all in her section.

At a table next to mine but in another waitress's section were four men who were just finishing their meal. I couldn't help but notice their waitress and compare her to mine—what a study in contrasts. Their waitress was slow, dull and inattentive to her customers. From the way she looked and acted, I figured she had just had a root canal or was scheduled for one the next morning. The men finished their meal and she eventually cleaned off the table. When one of the men asked her what she had for dessert, her response was a classic example of how *not* to do it. In her sad monotone she replied, "All we have left is some apple pie." What man in his right mind would order some "all we have left" kind of apple pie?

They tipped stingily and left.

After finishing my enjoyable meal I asked my vivacious little waitress the same question, "What do you have for dessert?" She stood erect, placed her hands on her hips and most convincingly said, "Hot apple pie, fresh out of the oven! Would you like some ice cream on that?" What hungry man in his right mind could pass up that kind of apple pie—with ice cream? Not only did she sell a piece of apple pie, she sold some ice cream. What a difference the use of basic salesmanship can make in running a business or any organization. It can also make a difference in the way we run our lives.

Veal Tonight?

City Café was situated downtown in a small town just off the main highway south of Memphis in rural Mississippi. To get a parking place outside or a seat inside you had best get there early for lunch. It was known for miles around as the place to get home-cooked, tasty vegetables. It takes a hard working, hungry man to swallow mashed potatoes dished out by most restaurants but his were properly buttered, salted and peppered. They went down easy. Most restaurant cooks don't know the first thing about making good biscuits and cornbread. Not so at City Café. The owner would comb the surrounding county in his search for elderly ladies with experience making fluffy biscuits and tasty cornbread. In the fifties nobody counted calories and nobody had ever heard of cholesterol. We just appreciated good cooking and enjoyed "pigging out," with no regard for the consequences.

The owner, Mr. Gantry, was a huge man with a booming voice and only one arm. His left arm was off at the elbow but he didn't seem to know it. He would usually hang out around the cash register because he knew that was where the money was, but now and then he would put on a show as he paraded among the tables telling tall tales to his guests, that nub of a left arm moving in unison with his right arm—dinner theater, hillbilly style. If guests came in that he didn't recognize he would leave his perch at the cash register and personally take their orders.

As I was dining one night Mr. Gantry was in rare form and we were enjoying his antics. A couple entered that he didn't know, so he proceeded to give them his version of the red carpet treatment. Mr. Gantry learned the couple was from "up North," was traveling south and was staying at the local motel. He was doubly pleased that the desk clerk at the motel had spoken kindly of City Café. He personally took their order. They each ordered veal from the menu.

Mr. Gantry returned to his perch at the cash register

and the waitress eventually served the couple. After a few minutes the man signaled Mr. Gantry over to his table. Mr. Gantry, of course, was expecting the man to be complimentary about the food, but this time he was to be disappointed. That fellow had obviously wallowed that piece of meat all over his plate trying to cut it, all to no avail. The man explained that the meat was as tough as a shoe sole—was he sure it was veal?

Mr. Gantry suddenly found himself forced into a defensive posture and he didn't handle it well. He assured the man that just three days ago that piece of meat was following the cow around in the pasture. That fellow just placed his knife and fork on his plate, folded his hands in his lap, looked up at Mr. Gantry and said loudly enough for all of us to hear, "I don't doubt that piece of meat just three days ago was following the cow around in the pasture. My question is, was it looking for milk?"

"Deducts" and the Cotton

During the 1940s and 1950s huge cotton plantations still existed in the Mississippi Delta and in the Black Prairie Belt of Mississippi. Some of these sprawling farms had thousands of acres of cotton land under cultivation with as many as fifty small tenant shacks that the workers lived in. Tenants were known as "sharecroppers," which meant that they farmed a designated plot of land using the landowner's animals and equipment. The landowner in turn would get half of the cotton produced on the piece of land. The plantation was anchored around the plantation store or "commissary" as it was sometimes called. Nearby would be the owner's plantation home and his own cotton gin. The plantation store would "furnish" the tenants all their needs during the year and at the end of the harvest in the fall each tenant would "settle up" with the landowner at the store.

These plantation stores stocked everything from horse collars to fatback to aspirin tablets. Shallow wall shelves reached fifteen feet or more in height. Ladders along the walls moved on rollers along rails and made the higher shelves reachable to clerks who, using broom handles with hooks mounted in the end, prided themselves in the art of hooking and flipping cans of pork and beans or sardines off the higher shelves, and catching them before they hit the floor. The manager and his bookkeepers would have an office in the middle of the store, sufficiently elevated to enable the manager to see all over the store. Out front a roof overhang across the front created a porch of sorts. Weather-beaten wooden benches stretched the length of the porched area. The carvings of generations of sitters with their Barlow knives were evident on the benches.

It was a warm sunny day when I parked out in the front of this plantation store, exited my car and started walking toward the entrance. A crowd of black youngsters huddled around an elderly black man seated on a bench caught my attention. The old man was obviously telling a tale that had the youngsters riveted.

As I drew closer, I could see the old fellow seated on the bench, hunched forward with his legs crossed and his left elbow resting on his knee. In his right hand he held a Barlow knife he was using to slowly add some more carvings to the old wooden bench. A heavy shock of gray hair was trying to crawl out from underneath a faded Cardinals baseball cap he had pulled down low over his eyes. Though he appeared to be staring at the ground, it was to become evident that he was aware of my presence and elevated his voice enough that I could hear what he was saying.

When I heard the old man tell the youngsters that the ducks got all his cotton last year, I slowed my pace so as to hear the rest of the story. I had spent my youth on a hill country cotton farm and had witnessed our cotton crop being devastated by boll weevils, boll worms and by weather extremes, but I had never heard before of ducks eating cotton. I, too, had become riveted and was fiddling around that porch killing enough time that I could hear the rest of what he was going to say. The old man continued telling how he had harvested his cotton, had it ginned and went to the office to "settle up." He said the landlord "deduct" an amount for this and "deduct" an amount for that, and when the landlord had finished with the settlement "deducts" had gotten all his crop. The old man then slowly rose to his feet, took off that old baseball cap and started to slap his legs with it as he laughed. I realized I had "been took" and could do nothing but join him.

Two Sacks Are Better Than One

Sleepy little Vardaman, Mississippi, can be pure pleasure to the traveler who finds it his lot to spend some time there. The town is chock-full of good people with big hearts. For many years it has been known as the "Sweet

Potato Capital of the South," and it celebrates each year with its Potato Festival. Big name stars are brought in to perform—a gala time is had by all.

On my many trips to Vardaman I have heard some amusing stories. The following is one of my favorites.

Many years ago a railroad company built a spur line to the town. This, of course, was a dead end line and when a train pulled in it simply had to back out when it was ready to leave. On the day the first train was to pull in, crowds gathered from all over the county to witness the big event. Some of these people only came to town once a year—some had never seen a train before.

Crowds of people were pressed in close on both sides of the track where the train was to stop. One man standing between the rails, shading his eyes with his hand, looking far down the rails shouted loud enough for all to hear, "I see it! It's a'coming!" Excitement welled up in the crowd as that train got closer and louder.

Soon that big engine slowed to a stop between the two lines of nervous onlookers. The engine was much bigger than they had expected—it literally towered over them. Then without warning, that big steam engine hissed loudly and spewed clouds of steam out between the legs of the nervous crowd. At this point in time some fun-loving wise guy made his move. He cupped his hands to his mouth and shouted as loudly as he could, "Look out, folks! This thing is fixing to turn around!"

Versions of just how many people were trampled that day in the cow pasture differ, but they all agreed that the pandemonium in that cow pasture would make a British soccer game of today look like a Sunday School picnic.

I cannot leave Vardaman without telling a story in

45

which I was the victim. These big-hearted, fun-loving people cherished the opportunity to pull a prank on young salesmen wearing white shirts, ties and shiny shoes.

It was a sultry day in August when I pulled into town. I had been drinking too many soda pops, and as I parked in front of this store and got out of my car, I noticed the desire to relieve myself was coming on strong. There was no public restroom in the whole town. The nearest ones were in a larger town eight miles distant, and there was no way I could make it that far. I entered the store, spoke to the manager and moved hurriedly to the back of the building. Desperation was setting in. I asked an employee what they did when they had to "wee-wee." He told me they simply got a small brown paper bag and used it for a container, then tossed it out the back door. I could see what appeared to be dozens of spent brown paper bags out back so I believed him. He brought me a small brown paper bag and I hid myself behind a stack of mule feed in the back of the store and did exactly as he had instructed me. I marveled at the way the brown paper bag stood up under the circumstances. However, I never had the opportunity to toss the bag out the back door. Just as that sack began to fill, the bottom fell out of it and my pretty shiny shoes and my sharply creased pants legs were saturated by the deluge. That's when I realized that I had an audience all the while, made up of store employees. All were delighted that a salesman had "been took," as they put it.

Incidentally, the trick is to use not one paper sack, but two (one inside the other). This arrangement of sacks will hold liquid for hours.

Surprise! Surprise!

In small rural southern towns in the fifties a peculiar kinship oftentimes existed between the grocery stores and the funeral homes. Families that owned funeral homes would also be in the grocery business, or grocery store owners would own shares in funeral homes. Employees of both would be shifted back and forth between the two businesses. Some of the best stories I ever heard were told by funeral home employees hanging around in grocery stores when they had nothing else to do—when nobody was dying.

Mr. "B" was a pudgy, portly old gentleman who sold fifty cents' per week burial insurance around town. He had a flair for short-sleeved white shirts, red ties and an oversize felt hat with the brim turned up all around. To see him "duck-walking" the streets you would think him to be cocky and arrogant. The opposite was true—he possessed a quiet demeanor. He was a natural when it came to talking to people about their upcoming deaths. He was good at what he did.

Late each afternoon Mr. "B" would turn in his paperwork at the funeral home office and inquire if there were any bodies upstairs under sheets. If so, he would mount the stairs, lift the sheet and view the corpse even if he didn't know who it was. One day the workers in the home decided to have a bit of fun with Mr. "B." One of them went upstairs, lay down on the table as though a corpse and the other workers carefully tucked the sheet around him. Mr. "B" came in shortly and, as usual, inquired as to whether there were any bodies upstairs. Upon being told there was one, he gingerly mounted the stairs and tripped lightly over to the sheet-covered body. As he lifted the sheet to peer under it, that fellow came up off that table, screamed and grabbed Mr. "B" by the shoulders. Mortal fear converted the diminutive Mr. "B" into a giant of a man. He tore himself loose, bolted down the stairs, got into his car and hurried home—to change his pants.

Another funeral home worker told me about his being confined to the small local hospital after having hemorrhoidal surgery. The bathroom was a separate room situated between his room and the room next to his which was occupied by a sophisticated little lady who was recovering from some malady. Part of his therapy was to sit in a tub of hot water several times each day. On one of his soakings he neglected to lock the door going into the other patient's room. He had no more than gotten undressed and slid down into that tub of hot water when the little lady burst in and found herself standing by the tub. Being a perfect gentleman, he stood up and shook hands with her.

He Who Laughs Last . . .

Sales forces with large corporations must undergo constant and continuous training. Changes in the economy as well as changes in demographics and in consumer buying habits mean that if you are still doing it the way you did it ten years ago, it is probably wrong. It is necessary that the finished product move into the hand of the consumer if the factory wheels are to keep turning and the flow of merchandise is to continue through the pipelines of the distribution system. Though sales and marketing techniques are forever being reorganized, there is one constant: human nature. It always has been, is now and always will be the same.

Techniques to get the buyer's attention are still the same. Tell him something he wants to hear and he will listen to you. Even the toughest and meanest buyer in the territory has his "button," which if pushed will gain his undivided attention. The trick is to find the button. If calling on a buyer that you have never called on before it is imperative that you check out his office décor as quickly as possible. What kind of pictures does he have on the walls or on his desk? What kind of lapel pin is he wearing? There is no effective presentation for a buyer who is simply being quiet when you talk—he must also be hearing what you are saying.

Mr. Chambers had his own wholesale grocery business and ran it with an iron fist. He was good to his salesmen and office personnel and they in turn were loyal to him. My problem with him was that he had never sold my line of detergents and cleaners, even though my products were the most powerful on the market. I had learned through some of his salesmen that Mr. Chambers had relatives who had stock in, and worked for, my primary competitor. As was to be expected, he was blindly loyal to them and sold their products only. My attempts to interview him were always thwarted by his office manager, a bald, pudgy and bespectacled little man who seemed to derive a deep seated pleasure from denying me access to Mr. Chambers.

I decided to write Mr. Chambers a personal letter letting him know when I would be in his area and explaining to him that I would appreciate it if he could give me a few minutes of his time. It must have worked. On my next trip the office manager did give me access to Mr. Chambers.

I walked into his office, we shook hands, exchanged the usual greetings and I took my seat across from him. His phone rang, giving me the opportunity to survey my surroundings. All four walls of his office had pictures of beautiful bird dogs on them, both setters and pointers. Eureka! I had found his "button." He finished his call, turned to me and I immediately began to talk about the pictures, bird dogs and bird hunting. His head dropped and he began to shuffle through the papers on his desk. He excused himself, made a phone call and called his secretary into the office. It was obvious that I had lost him. He was suddenly not interested in anything I had to say. I had done everything according to the book, exactly as I had been trained, and I had failed. I gathered my papers and left.

On my way out the door I came across the pudgy little office manager enjoying a smoke. He couldn't wait to ask me if I'd gotten the order. When I told him that I hadn't, he lit up as though he had just won the lottery. In my bewilderment I mentioned to "Pudgy" that I had noticed all those pictures of beautiful bird dogs on the walls of Mr. Chambers's office, and that he must be an avid bird hunter. "Oh," said the office manager, "that's not Mr. Chambers's office. He is just using that room while his office down the hall is being remodeled. Mr. Chambers hates dogs. He is more into horses."

Some months later Mr. Chambers became ill and passed away. His son-in-law took over the business and called me immediately, wanting to know when I could call on him—he wanted to order a carload of my detergents. I was waiting for him when he opened his office the next morning. On my way out I handed "Pudgy" a signed copy of an order for ten tons of my products. This time "Pudgy" was bewildered and I had the winning lottery ticket. He who laughs last . . .

The Bootlegger

It was a hot, humid day in July and all morning I had been combing the highways and byways of this rural Mississippi county trying to sell my customers more soap products than they wanted to buy. I was proud of my new company car. It was air-conditioned, and that was indeed special in the early fifties. However, the moving back and forth from my cool car to the heat and sultriness of my customers' offices and warehouses was beginning to tell on me. People were moving about, mopping their brows, fanning feverishly with their old straw hats and of course discussing the weather, specifically the heat. One elderly gentleman, holding his hat in his left hand and mopping his brow with the other, mentioned to me that the City Café on the town square now had air-conditioning. I immediately began to work my way in that direction for my noon meal.

I parked out front and made my way into the crowded café. The sweet fragrance of mustard greens, field peas, hot cornbread and fresh apple pie permeated the air. Pity the poor hungry man who has never in his life experienced such! I took a seat at the only vacant table and a middle-aged, oversized waitress waddled over to take my order. What felt like a stiff April breeze kept fanning my hair and blowing my napkin off the table.

Then I spotted the source—an air-conditioning unit standing against the wall opposite me as big as two bales of cotton, one stacked atop the other. That massive unit was shaking and whirring as it struggled to cool the place down a bit.

I noticed a very well-dressed man obviously looking for a place to sit so I invited him to join me. He looked me in the eye and gave me a warm smile as he shook my hand firmly and took a seat at my table. The man was wearing very expensive clothes. He had a diamond stick-pin in his tie and was wearing a ring with a diamond in it as big as a cat's eye. My lucky day—this man just had to be the mayor, a lawyer, a doctor or a preacher. He was an intelligent conversationalist. He said all the right things. His mannerisms were flawless. I couldn't help but think what a great salesman he could be. He had not told me what kind of business he was in, but I had to know, so I asked him. He responded confidently and matter-of-factly that he was the local bootlegger—that he made his living selling whiskey. I promptly dropped my fork. In those days decent folks avoided fraternizing with bootleggers like they avoided the plague, and here was I, the sales representative of a large corporation, breaking bread with one openly! He seemed amused at my reaction and began to put me at ease with his skillful manipulation of the flow of conversation. He did seem a bit defensive when he made the point that he served a sophisticated clientele. Some of his best customers, he said, were the best dressed ladies on the street outside, the ones I would surely tip my hat to. When I had finished eating, I told him truthfully that I had enjoyed visiting with him.

Later that day I was to get "the rest of the story" from one of my customers. The bootlegger was a well-liked man in the area. He contributed generously to all worth-while causes. He was one of the largest contributors to both the local churches. His home was one of the nicest ones in town and he was well liked by his neighbors. And the fact that his brother-in-law was the mayor didn't hurt him any.

One oft-repeated story about the man concerned a young preacher who was new in town. The preacher apparently had not been made aware of the bootlegger's sizable contribution to his church's budget every year and had set out to bring him to justice. The young man went to the bootlegger's house one night and bought a pint of Jim Beam so as to have the goods on him. However, on his way to the police department he himself was picked up and charged with possession. The deacons had a little problem with this one but were able to work it out.

For some time it bore heavily on my mind that this most interesting man, blessed with God-given graces, intelligent, and possessing exceptional talent chose to make a career of selling illegal whiskey. Certainly he could have been extremely successful in any legitimate field of endeavor. What a waste of brain power—what a tragedy.

Lemon Pie Up Your Nose

Having called on my last customer in Carrollton, I drove out to the highway and headed to my motel room in Winona, about eight miles away. As I traveled east on the two-lane highway, I found myself behind an old jalopy traveling in the same direction but in the middle of the road astride the white center line. The driver of the old jalopy was obviously deep into the juice of the grape—he was driving considerably under the speed limit and was zig-zagging back and forth across that white center line.

My attempts to pass him were thwarted when each time I started around he would "zig" instead of "zag." Oncoming cars were just plain lucky to zip on by when he was in his "zag." Traffic began to stack up behind me as we all slowed down and followed at a safe distance rather than chance trying to pass him during his "zig."

Eventually we got into Winona and the old jalopy began to slow its pace, eventually stopping dead still in the center of the highway in front of the Bus Station Café. That poor drunk got out of his car, stumbled and staggered to the front door of the café and disappeared inside. My motel was directly across the street from the café, so I pulled into the motel and parked in front of my room. Curiosity possessed me—I had to know what had happened to the poor guy.

As I crossed the street to the café, I noticed his old car still standing in the middle of the highway with traffic moving both ways around it. On entering the café I spotted the drunk sitting on a stool and hanging onto the counter with both hands to keep from falling off. As his head kept moving around and around, he told the waitress to bring him a piece of lemon pie. She reluctantly placed the lemon pie and a fork on the counter in front of him. He eventually got a proper grip of that fork and began to stab away at the piece of lemon pie. On the third stab, he got some pie on his fork and started toward his mouth with it. The problem was that as his head continued to move around and around, he missed his mouth and stuck most of that bite of pie up his nose.

About that time the drunk felt a tap on his right shoulder. He turned his head and looked up into the face of a burly policeman who was shaking his head from side to side as he half lifted the drunk off his stool, half carried him to the patrol car and delivered him to the "pokey." As the two went out the door I overheard the kind policeman ask the poor drunk in a low voice, where did he think he was going in the shape he was in? The drunk responded simply that he had figured on going to Winona if that white line held out.

Turnip Greens Today?

It seems that the more effective salesmen I have known have succeeded in developing their skills to the point that they employ them not only on the job, but in every area of their lives. These same people seem to always have good marriages and well-rounded children. I'm also convinced that these people and their families have fewer health problems. It is a known fact that the body chemistry of a positive and happy person is more balanced. Our relationships with all the people around us can be so much more pleasant when we work at fine tuning and using these sales skills. Nothing is as contagious as a joyous frame of mind in a gathering of people. Nothing seems to brighten up a room full of people like the sudden entrance of another person with a cheerful disposition, a positive outlook and a genuine concern for others.

A customer and I were sitting in his little office one morning discussing these very things. He had a young son just beginning what he hoped would be a career in sales and was interested in anything I might have to say.

Mr. Milner's office was situated in the front of the store with glass-enclosed sides and was slightly elevated. From his chair he had a panoramic view of both the inside of the store and the entire parking lot area. This particular morning was cold, blustery and rainy. As we talked we noticed an older model pick-up truck had parked on the more distant part of the parking lot. The old fellow driving kept on blowing his horn and looking up toward the store. Mr. Milner became quite concerned after a while and decided he had best check on the situation.

He dug an old raincoat out from under a stack of newspapers, put it over his head and, holding it with both hands, hurried across the parking lot and down to the old man in the truck. In no time at all he was hurrying back toward the store, hanging on to that raincoat as the cold wind tried to tear it away from him. On entering the office he removed that raincoat and flung it down in the corner. This good man that I had never before, in many years of calling on him, seen emotionally upset was flushed with anger. I could swear that I saw little puffs of smoke coming out of his ears. I sat quietly as he turned toward me, no doubt reflecting on the course of our conversation prior to his trip down to that truck. Suddenly he blurted out, "Do you know what that old man wanted? He wanted to know if I wanted to buy some turnip greens!"

The Road to Riches

Jack and Barney were a couple of happy-go-lucky brothers who had spent all their working years in the grocery industry. Jack had worked as a supermarket butcher and Barney had experience at every other level of responsibility in the same store. Both were very good at what they did. Both were hard-working, honest, extroverted and well liked. All these qualities, plus the fact that they employed basic sales skills every day without even realizing it, made them natural candidates for a business of their own.

A local banker casually mentioned to them over coffee one morning that they should begin to consider going into their own business. They had for years been making money for someone else—why not make some for themselves? The seed had been planted and Jack's and Barney's fever began to rise. They put out feelers to their suppliers, distributors, vendors and sales representatives as to their desires.

Sooner than they had expected, word came to them that the only supermarket in a small town just twenty miles away was for sale. Financing was no problem for them. In short order Jack and Barney were the proud proprietors of their very own supermarket. Jack took over the meat market operation and Barney handled the other duties. They were smart enough to know the lines of responsibility needed to be clearly defined between the two of them. This they did and their business began to grow. They were especially pleased when they would notice customers shopping in their store who had driven the twenty miles from their home town just to give their old friends some of their business.

Jack and Barney were for the first time in their lives beginning to enjoy a degree of prosperity. The trouble was that they were beginning to have a problem with this newfound prosperity. Both had developed an affinity for the juice of the grape. Jack had become an authority on every brand of beer in his cooler. In the jargon of the pool room, he had become a "guzzler." Suddenly bills were coming due and the brothers were having trouble paying them on time. Their business was still growing but their good times expenditures were growing faster. Jack had begun to sneak a beer now and then on the job. His business decisions were noticeably less quick and crisp.

To Jack and Barney I was an old man—I had two sons about their age. These two men were so special to me that I had decided on my next call that I would attempt to reason with them. Maybe I could get their undivided attention and help them to see their problem, accept the fact that they had it, and start to do something about it.

On my next call I was able to get Jack isolated in his little office, just the two of us, one on one. I closed the door, eliminating all outside stimuli. Jack showed me the courtesy of giving me his undivided attention as I began my lecture. It was my belief that the root cause of his financial problem was that he was drinking too much beer. If he could just get this under control, the brothers would in very short order be banking more money than they had ever dreamed of. Jack leaned forward in his chair and seemed to be absorbing my every word. I was convinced that I was reaching him. I was feeling good about my efforts.

My feathers were to fall, however, when Jack interrupted. "Mr. Carter, when I close this store every day I go by Miss Annie's Saloon and drink a six-pack of beer. Then by the time I get home I'm the richest S.O.B. in town!"

The Old Man

At this time in my career I had customers with whom I'd been doing business for over thirty years. Older customers had either retired or passed their businesses on to younger people. Far too many had themselves passed on. I, myself, was beginning to move and think a lot more slowly. Time lines were beginning to mark my face and I was losing my hair. I had come to the point in my life that I had to face the reality that middle age had come and gone. Aging gracefully was what other people were supposed to do. Now each morning when I faced the mirror I was reminded of the fact that the aging process was a reality in my life. The important thing for me to do was accept it and set about handling it as gracefully as possible.

The first customer I called on this particular day kidded me about my thinning hair. He even offered to get me a good price on a hairpiece through a friend of his. Throughout the remainder of the day it seemed I was being subjected to more and more good-natured jokes about my age. One young fellow, no doubt coached to do so, asked if I had ever personally met Abe Lincoln. A kid told me that he sure wouldn't want to be old and gray-headed like me. Edgily I countered that I wouldn't exactly cherish the idea of being young and ignorant like him.

So it went throughout the remainder of the day. Then on my last call of the day I was to be subjected to the crowning insult. I had parked across the street from my customer's business. As I got out of my car and started across the street I noticed a car parked in front on the store with four loud and rowdy youngsters in it. The windows in the car were down and they could be heard a block away as they bounced around in that car. They were climbing back and forth over the seats, jumping up and down and doing all the things I would never permit my children to do. As I walked alongside their car they suddenly became quiet and still. One small boy on the back seat on the side next to me was huddled down, very still and very quiet. He was looking up at me and when our eyes met, he said simply, "Hey, old man!"

Nine months later I took early retirement.

The Acquisition of Knowledge

After leaving the hills of northeast Mississippi and serving in the Air Force during World War II, I calculated the surest way to land a job with a car and expenses was to take advantage of the G.I. Bill and go to college. Hence I found myself enrolled as a freshman at "Ole Miss." I was also to find out shortly that not all the learning on campus was to come from the textbooks afforded by the G.I. Bill. The student body ranged all the way from the very wealthy down to folks like me, and the behavior patterns of the rich kids sometimes made me lose sleep. There were very few cars on campus, and after seeing a rich kid lose his new car in a crap game one night I couldn't sleep. But the next Monday he came back on campus driving another new one.

The dormitories on campus were two-story structures with hallways extending the length of the building and bathrooms located at the ends of each floor. Rooms were directly opposite each other with doors opening into the rooms. Each room had its own lavatory and mirror but no commode or shower.

Freshmen, of course, were the victims of the unbridled hazing taking place. "Melon Head" Morris was the kind of kid that upper classmen just loved to pick on. He must have weighed 250 pounds and was always eating something sweet and calorie-laden as he huffed and puffed his way around. Shortly after the end of the war, sugar and chocolate had again become available and Melon Head was delighted. He could eat six chocolate bars at a sitting, and his most favorite thing to eat was the new chocolate chip doughnut.

Some of the fellows on the floor came up with a whole new level of hazing and poor Melon Head was to be the victim. They purchased a box of glazed donuts and a box of Ex-Lax. They broke the laxative up into little chips that looked and tasted exactly like chocolate chips. Then they punched little holes in the donuts, pushed the chips of chocolate-tasting laxative inside and reheated the donuts so as to reglaze the exterior. Melon Head was deeply appreciative of their generosity when they offered him four of the donuts. He was licking his chops as he went into his room and closed the door behind him. The other fellows quickly tied a piece of rope securely to his doorknob and stretched it tightly across the hall where they tied it equally as securely to the doorknob directly opposite. Then they sat down to wait.

After about an hour, stirrings could be heard in Melon Head's room as he tried with no success to get his door open and go down the hall to the bathroom. He moaned, groaned and begged for someone to open his door but nobody seemed to be listening. Eventually someone did untie the rope and let Melon Head outside. He spent two days in the infirmary getting flushed out and another day cleaning up his room.

A Bad Day

Some days in the life of a salesman, the same as in the life of a lawyer, preacher or carpenter, are much worse than other days. This was one of those days. My mail the day before did not include a notice about the raise I was expecting but it did include a notice that a valued customer was much too late in paying an invoice for a carload of my soap products. Rumor was that he was expected to declare bankruptcy. Copies of invoices received in the same mail revealed that two carloads of soap products that were scheduled to be shipped before the end of the month were actually invoiced after the first, making me behind on quota for that month. On top of all this I was forced to pack up and leave my wife alone with a small son who was obviously coming down with something. A bad day indeed.

All these matters were bearing down on me as I drove north on Highway 45 toward Aberdeen. Suddenly and without warning a huge brown dog leaped out of the ditch and into the path of my car. There was no way I could avoid hitting the animal. After a sickening thud I glanced into my rearview mirror and witnessed that dog's body spinning round and round before catapulting into the grassy ditch. As a dog lover I felt sick inside. I figured the right thing to do was to turn around, go back to that little farmhouse I passed and express my regrets. I pulled up into a gravel driveway, got out of my car, walked up onto that old creaky porch and knocked on the door.

There was no response at the door but out of the corner of my eye I detected movement coming around the corner of the house. The movement I saw turned out to be a little old lady wearing an old-fashioned sunbonnet and an ankle-length flowing skirt. She was holding a pitchfork like a javelin and without a word was charging me with it. Adding to my problem was the fact that she had positioned herself between me and my car. She was obviously in no mood to negotiate so I bolted off the end of the porch opposite where my car was parked and started to run around the rear of the house with her in hot pursuit. I scattered a flock of Rhode Island Reds that were pecking around in the back yard. She tripped over one of the scattering chickens and gave me the edge I needed to get into my car, lock it, crank it and get it going. As I sped away I caught a glimpse of her still charging after me through the dust and flying gravel. The remainder of the day simply had to be better.

The good news is that a month later as I was passing this same house (I didn't bother to stop) I glanced into her yard and saw the little old lady digging around her flowers. Plain to see was a pitchfork propped against the porch and that big brown dog with a heavily splinted left rear leg hobbling along behind her.

"Dog—Gone"

I was one of six children who grew up on a farm during the Great Depression. We were very poor, but didn't know the difference because everybody else was in the same boat. It was decades later that, upon reflection, I realized that we were blessed with a God-fearing father and mother who loved us equally and dearly.

Dad was a stern disciplinarian. Two things that were absolutely forbidden were drinking and cussing. I was to learn about the latter one day when as a youngster he took me out with a single-barrel shotgun to teach me how to kill rabbits. We hadn't tramped very far into the woods when all of a sudden there was a big rabbit sitting in his nest. I was so excited that I blurted out "G—D—!" I had never used this expletive before and still can't understand why I used it then as a young kid. Dad reached over and took that shotgun, put the safety on and lay it on the ground. He then broke off a fair sized limb from a bush, grabbed me by the shoulder and gave me a tail-whipping that I never forgot. That rabbit took advantage of the situation, and so far as I know, is still running.

My younger brother, growing up in this disciplined atmosphere, had gotten into the habit of using the strongest superlative he could get away with. Anytime he heard or saw something profound he would say, "Dog-Gone!" Later on I was to serve a hitch in the Air Force, finish college and get a "traveling job," as it was commonly called. My younger brother liked the idea of being able to drive a shiny new car every year, stay in motels and eat in good restaurants, all at company expense. Later on he found a job as a sales representative and moved to Montgomery, Alabama. He and his wife settled in a house in a pleasant neighborhood where the neighbors all chatted and walked their dogs.

One sweet little old lady walked her little dog down the sidewalk by my brother's house late each afternoon. As time passed, she began to stop and chat with my brother and his wife as she came by. Of course, the little dog was often the subject of conversation. One afternoon she came down the sidewalk as usual, but didn't have her little dog. My brother immediately asked her if the dog was sick. The little lady stared at the ground, teared up and began to tell her sad story. She detailed how she was walking her little dog down a street two blocks over when a huge, strange dog lunged out from behind some bushes, quickly killed her little dog, dragged it off and apparently ate it. To my brother, this was indeed profound and he had to come up with his strongest superlative. You guessed it—"Dog-Gone!"

Little Toe Broken

Good salesmen and good hitters have something in common—both are born with a degree of capability but must work constantly throughout their careers to better themselves. Now and then they must reflect on their past performance, look at their successes and their failures and seek to learn from both. Time flies and things fluctuate. Conditions in the business world are constantly changing and the successful salesman must adapt quickly to these changes.

One of the first things a new salesman has to learn is that the buyer is usually a busy man, and getting his undivided attention requires some skills. With most buyers this simply means telling him something he wants to hear. The salesman's mother-in-law may have just moved in with him, his best bird dog may have just been run over by a truck, he may have a bad back problem or a splitting headache, but the buyer couldn't care less. However, that Band-Aid covered scratch on *his* forearm is a mountainous issue to him—dwell on it. Every man or woman alive likes to talk about his or her own children, grandchildren or their new car. However they may begin to yawn quickly if you begin to talk about *yours*. Simply put, tell the man enough of what he wants to hear to get his undivided attention and then deliver the body punch.

Early on in my career I was trying to be careful to use every skill I had been taught thus far. While walking around in my house barefooted I had accidentally kicked a door and broken the little toe of my right foot. The next day the entire foot was swollen and had turned black. On this same day I had to call on one of my wholesalers in a nearby town. I hobbled into the warehouse area for an inventory check and, as usual, ran into "Charlie," the warehouse manager. Charlie was a good-natured, burly black man with a toothy smile that stretched from underneath his left ear all the way across his face to underneath his right ear. If Charlie had ever had a bad moment, it didn't show. He inquired at once about my foot problem and I explained how I had accidentally kicked a door facing and broken my little toe. When he told me that he had broken his little toe in the exact same way, it opened the door for me to employ some of my newly acquired skills. I knew it was time for me to divert attention away from *my* broken toe to his. In my clumsy attempt to do this I asked Charlie if *his* foot turned black.

66

The Hitchhiker

As I traveled the roads of Mississippi back in the fifties, it seems, in retrospect, there were many more "legitimate" hitchhikers than today. Unlike today, motorists had no fear of giving one a lift. They usually carried a small greasy bag, and in summer time were rather greasy and smelly themselves, but this didn't matter since we had no air conditioning in our cars and rode with the windows open. They usually weren't going anywhere in particular—they would just bum a ride to wherever you happened to be going. Often you would later see them hitchhiking back to where they came from. They just enjoyed the ride and the conversation. Surprisingly, some of them were very well informed—especially about politics.

One such hitchhiker more or less headquartered in "Donkey" McGee's store (more about "Donkey" later). He was known simply as "Pete," and he would make several trips daily between Winona and Kosciusko, gleaning tidbits of knowledge from everyone he rode with. He always carried a small greasy bag and the contents of that bag was a matter of much conjecture among the locals. Some even said they had peeped inside it and it was full of twenty-dollar bills. My guess was that it had cheese, crackers and pork and beans in it. One local claims that he passed Pete up one morning on his way to Kosciusko, but when he got to Kosciusko, the first man he saw was Pete, drinking a cup of coffee someone had bought for him.

Political fever was running high in Mississippi. Elections were just around the corner. Sam Lumpkin, along with other candidates, was running for governor, and happened to be traveling from Winona to Kosciusko on this particular day. Old Pete was standing on the side of the road with that greasy bag in his left hand and his right thumb stuck out, begging for a lift.

Sam Lumpkin eased over on the shoulder, opened the passenger door for Pete and without introducing himself began talking politics. Sam was amazed at Pete's knowledge of the candidates running for office in the on-going campaign—so much so that he began to ask Pete questions about different candidates. Of course Sam was primarily interested in the governor's race and wanted to know how Pete felt about his opponents. In each case Pete would give what Sam considered to be a very intelligent analysis of each candidate's situation, what section of the state each would carry, which segment of the vote they would receive, and so on. Finally Sam couldn't stand it any longer.

"How do you think Sam Lumpkin is going to do?"

Without a moment's hesitation Pete answered. "He won't get a damned smell." And he didn't.

Adios, Comrade!

In the mid to late 1940s the Communist Party was feverishly propounding the teachings of Marx and Lenin to anyone who would listen. College campuses, with their overflowing student bodies of young intellectuals, were supposed to be fertile grounds for recruitment to the Party. A young, dedicated Communist student would be planted on a campus with the primary objective of creating a cell around himself, hoping to eventually build a movement that would be influential on campus. "Mike" was the obvious plant on the Ole Miss Campus.

Mike, of Polish extraction, had a last name that no one could articulate. My effort to pronounce his name sounded more like a sneeze. He had grown up in a northern city as part of a large family, all of whom worked at a local steel mill. The transition from that environment to the environment that existed on the Ole Miss campus at the time was considerable, but young Mike handled it well. He stayed out of trouble, attended his classes and made good grades. He also subscribed to the Communist newspaper, *The Daily Worker*, and tried to get every student in the dorm to read its ridiculous content. His instructions from the Party were to parrot the party line at every opportunity, and this he did. He had become so obnoxious that a group of students asked for and got an audience with the chancellor to discuss a way to get rid of him. The chancellor explained to the students that Mike was not engaged in any activity that could be considered illegal. They would simply have to tolerate him. The student group came away disappointed but determined to take matters into their own hands.

In those days freshmen who were not veterans were subjected to severe hazing that would no longer be permitted on campus. About eight miles out of town on the Batesville highway was a gravel road leading about a half mile out into the wooded hills to a vacant little country shack. The lights of Oxford were clearly visible from the front porch of the shack, but two obstacles lay between. In the edge of the yard was a tightly stretched electric fence about eighteen inches off the ground and just beyond the fence was a steep ravine about twenty feet deep. Selected freshmen were told that a lovely girl, "Jean," lived in the house along with her father, a huge and violent man who wouldn't hesitate to kill any student he found messing around with his daughter. The father was supposedly a night watchman in Batesville and was never home until about one A.M. Hence Jean happily entertained young freshmen anytime prior to midnight.

Two upperclassmen would convince a freshman to go out to see Jean with them. On the way out to the shack they would constantly remind the freshman that Jean's father was a mean and violent man, but that he would not be home since he worked in Batesville at night. A third member of the hazing team would already be in position inside the shack with a twelve-gauge double-barreled shotgun. The victim and the other two members of the hazing team would walk up on the porch, knock on the door and call out to Jean. The fellow inside would stomp the floor as though getting out of bed, bellow loudly that he was fixing to kill him some college boys. Before the three fellows could get off the porch the one inside fired one barrel of that shotgun and one of the three fell as though shot. As the other two raced across the yard, the second blast came from that shotgun and the second boy fell to the ground as though shot. By this time the victim would be heading full steam toward the lights of Oxford. After tripping over that strand of electric fence and cutting a couple of cartwheels he would disappear into the ravine. The bottom of that ravine was covered with loafers that frantic freshmen had left behind.

The fellows devised a scheme to get rid of "Comrade" Mike that included a trip out to see Jean. Surprisingly,

Mike fell for it right away and the plan was put into effect immediately. My roommate had an old surplus army Jeep, so he and I went out early, along with several other students, just to observe. It was a cold, damp December night with a pale moon faintly peeking through a light cloud cover. We hid our Jeep and lay prone on the cold ground to watch the proceedings. The fellows bringing "Comrade" Mike out felt it necessary to change the plan a bit. Instead of letting him run away into that ravine, they had three other friends in position to tackle him as he ran.

Everything worked as planned as they tackled him and pinned him to the ground. Then they removed Mike's shoes, socks, pants and underwear, leaving him clad only in a T-shirt. I remember thinking the T-shirt must have come from a discount store—it only reached to his navel. As they held Mike down, flat on his back, two fellows pretending to be Jean's brothers towered over him. One of them had a hunting knife and was sharpening it on a brick as they discussed the procedure for relieving him of certain parts of his anatomy. Mike was moaning, begging, and crying but the man with the knife seemed unimpressed. At this point "Comrade" Mike, the dedicated Communist, an avowed atheist, did something that surprised all of us—he started praying to a God he did not profess to believe in. When the chips were down Marx and Lenin were no help at all. My roommate and I could no longer take it and exited the scene. The fellow with the knife, of course, did not follow through, but did extract a promise from Mike that he would leave campus immediately and never return. Still fresh in my memory is the sound of Mike's big bare feet slapping the hard-packed gravel as he raced away toward the highway. My roommate and I gathered his clothes and his glasses and went along the country road calling out to him. After an hour or so of searching for Mike to no avail, we returned to our dormitory. The first person we saw was Mike, still clad in his discount store T-shirt, sitting down in a phone booth and talking to someone pretending to be the local sheriff. Apparently some understanding motorist had picked Mike up and brought him back to his dorm. We placed his clothes and his glasses outside his door and went to bed. The next morning "Comrade" Mike's room was empty and he was never seen on campus again.

"Till Death Do Us Part"

After being married to me over thirty years my wife was well aware of my strengths as well as my frailties. She knew that I enjoyed kidding people. She also knew that I only kidded the people I loved. For that reason she continued to stay married to me even though she was more often than not the butt of my jokes. Old country people would describe a husband and wife team that had successfully managed and built a family unit as one in which he would "push" and she would "scotch" for him. My wife knew how to "scotch."

As the years passed her health began to deteriorate but she continued to travel with me some. It became necessary for her to make stops along the way and take short walks while traveling. One afternoon late I stopped at a small station to gas up and suggested that she take care of her walking while I pumped gas and paid the man. The cashier was an elderly but portly little fellow, constantly on the move as he talked and tugged at his oversized jeans that were trying to slide down around his ankles. All the time I was paying him he was watching my wife as she scurried back and forth in his parking lot. I explained to him that it was necessary for her to walk frequently while traveling because of a health condition. In his clumsy attempt to be nice he reared back, raised up on his toes, hitched up his pants with both hands and said emphatically, "She walks pretty darned good to be as old as she is!" To me this was simply too rich to keep from her. It was a very long trip to the motel.

After a long night in the motel I arose early and went outside to walk some while my wife grabbed a few extra winks. I noticed on the front seat passenger side of a Mercedes parked nearby a huge dog was sitting stiffly upright with his head tilted slightly to his right as he stared out the window. On closer examination it was obvious that the dog was not moving, breathing or blinking his eyes. This was a beautifully stuffed and mounted animal that for reasons unknown to me the owner of the car kept beside him on the front seat.

It had already been a long afternoon and night—it might as well be a long day. I went back inside, woke my wife and told her there was a beautiful dog outside she just had to see. She got out of bed, slipped on her house shoes, put on her robe, pulled the collar up tight with both hands and stepped outside. I pointed out the Mercedes and she walked up alongside the passenger window. Immediately she began to talk all the "dog talk" she knew. Getting no response from that mounted dog, she scolded it for not responding and walked around in front of the car, put both hands on the hood, leaned forward and continued to "dog talk." The only sound she heard was me, rolling in the grass and struggling for breath. A *very* long day indeed.

Looking for Me?

Before there were McDonald's and Taco Bell—before there were Hardee's and Shoney's—before there were Morrison's and Quincy's, a hungry traveling man would most likely stop at a place called Grannie's Kitchen, Bill's Burgers, City Café or Monk's Place when a hunger pain grabbed him. A salesman would learn early on to pick an eating place that was covered up with the cars of locals during mealtime hours. There was always a good reason why locals didn't frequent an eating place. Upon entering a strange restaurant, it was always a good idea to visit the restroom—the kitchen would be just as clean or just as dirty as the restroom. I remember one restroom that I was checking out while standing at the urinal. I had never seen so much graffiti. All four walls and the ceiling were covered—some of it humorous but most of it vulgar and filthy. As I relieved myself at the urinal my eyes roamed the walls and even to the ceiling as I read the graffiti. Suddenly I was stopped abruptly at a message scrawled on the ceiling—"Why do you look up here for a joke when the real joke is in your hand?"

Monk's Place was situated in a remote area about one mile out of town. The place was no Waldorf but it did have the tastiest greasy burger in the area. Even then he always had onions that were as sweet as our Vidalias of today. A couple of his burgers and a "short" Coke, followed by two Tums, would help a hungry salesman make it to the next meal.

Monk's Place was converted into a restaurant from a small home. Customers would enter the front door into a small dining area with three tables and chairs. As one entered, directly in front was a bar stretching left to right with five bar stools. Behind the bar was a wall mirror that reflected anyone coming or going out the door to the bar customers. A hallway extended deeper into the building just to the left of the bar. Off this hallway were restrooms and private rooms where groups gathered to gamble and drink beer or booze. This, of course, was illegal at the time but to my knowledge Monk was never raided by the sheriff.

One night I was sitting at the bar with three other fellows enjoying a greasy burger, fries and a "short" Coke. The atmosphere was light as we all chatted and now and then glanced into the mirror to see who was entering the door behind us. The light atmosphere, however, changed to a dead hush when the biggest, meanest looking hombre I had ever seen made his entrance. This fellow was about six-foot-six, sported a Texas hat, cowboy boots and a belt buckle as big as a terrapin. In his right hand was the longest, shiniest pistol I had ever seen, and that cannon was pointed right at my backside. The way I had it figured, he was zeroed in just to the left of my backbone and between the third and fourth ribs. As mortal fear possessed me my lower jaw began to flop uncontrollably. My teeth were chattering so loudly that everyone in the place could hear. In my effort to stop the chattering, I placed my elbows on the bar and firmly positioned my flopping chin in my cupped hands. This didn't help—the top of my head then started to bounce up and down. By this time, the big fellow had looked us over, determined that we were not the one or ones he was looking for, and had disappeared down the hallway. Without a word, all four of us hit that front door at the same time. We later learned the man he was looking for was not in Monk's Place that night.

Man and the Moon

A typical day in the life of a salesman is one in which nothing seems to go as planned. Sometime during the day he will have to cool his heels unnecessarily while a buyer carries on an idle conversation with someone else. This someone else is oftentimes a local who has just dropped by for a friendly visit. You have a limited time to make this call and get to the next one before he closes for the day. Neither the buyer nor his visitor could care less about your schedule. They are just having an enjoyable visit together.

One day I was waiting outside a buyer's office while a local lawyer was visiting with him. The story I heard from the lawyer was worth waiting around to hear and tell about later.

It seems that this lawyer had just finished serving as the attorney for the accused in a local murder case. One young man had shot and killed another and there was one eyeball witness, an elderly black man. The old man hobbled around on a walking stick as he peered cautiously through his thick lenses. He obviously had visual impairments. The lawyer figured to cast doubt on the old man as a witness by exploiting his obvious visual problem. The old man felt his way into the witness chair and the lawyer began what he was sure would be a discrediting of the old man's testimony.

"Mr. Moses, did you actually see the accused shoot the victim?"

"Yes sir, I see'd him when he done it."

"How far away were you from the accused?"

"About fifty feet."

"Mr. Moses, you obviously have a problem with your eyes. Can you see twenty-five feet?"

"Yes sir, I can see that far."

"Can you see fifty feet?"

"Yes sir, I can see fifty feet."

"Mr. Moses, just how far can you see?" The lawyer said he knew he had lost the case when the old man pondered that question for a moment, then leaned his head back in his chair, rolled his eyes toward the ceiling and said, "Mr. Lawyer Man, on a clear night I can see all the way to the moon!"

A Better Way

Corporations like the one I worked for would frequently call their sales force together for a meeting. We would usually arrive at the meeting place late afternoon on the day before the meeting began, which was at eight o'clock the following morning. This afforded all of us the opportunity to socialize with other sales people the night before while we dined in a nice restaurant somewhere in the area. Being able to visit cities like Memphis, Jackson, New Orleans, Dallas, Atlanta or Cincinnati with expenses paid was a treat for all of us. However, come eight o'clock the following morning the party was over and it was all business.

Company sales meetings were expensive and there was always a good reason for having one. It could be a change in company policy, a change in a product or the introduction of a new product. Whatever the reason, the task before us as salespeople was laid out by our advertising people, production people or possibly our brand people. Once the responsibility of the sales force was clearly defined, we would break down into smaller groups to discuss how we were going to get the job done. Every man was given the opportunity to contribute and once a consensus was reached, each man had two options—he could either "get with the program" or "get his hat." Always we were looking for a better way to get the job done.

Frequently my mind would wonder at all the talk about "a better way." It seemed to me that all the progress in the world has resulted from reasonable people genuinely seeking a better way. I would reflect on my childhood during the Depression on a farm in the hill country of the South. I would watch my dad as he tried to get a stalk of corn to produce two ears rather than one, how he tried to get more pounds of cotton per acre, or how to get hens to lay more eggs. He couldn't have cared less about being a part of the search for a better way. During those hard times he was simply acting out of necessity.

My dad's searching for a better way apparently carried over to me. I remember how flocks of sparrows would swarm around in the hall of our barn after we had fed all the animals and chickens. It seemed to me the sparrows were getting more of the precious feed than the animals were. I would scare them off and they would return immediately. As I walked around in the muck in front of our barn it dawned on me that a better way to get rid of the sparrows might be to throw one of the soggy Mosby corn cobs under my feet through that barn hall. As it hurtled through the hall, changing ends, surely it would take out some sparrows. Little did I know the aborigines of Australia centuries before had come up with the same idea and it resulted in the boomerang.

I picked up a long, soggy Mosby corn cob and with all my strength I threw it through that barn hall into those sparrows. Unknown to me, my dad was behind the barn and just as I released that soggy corn cob he stepped out into the other end of the barn hall directly into its path. That cob caught him just above his left ear. His old felt hat went flying through the air and he dropped to his knees. He slowly rolled over, sat on the ground and leaned against the barn. Terrified, I rushed over and sat down beside him. Dad reached out with his long strong arm and hugged me close as he struggled to laugh through his pain. I joined him as I struggled to laugh through my tears.

Where Is the Post Office?

The town square in Houston looked very much like the town square in any other small town in rural Mississippi. Occupying the entire block was the courthouse, shade trees and long benches which in fair weather were filled with locals spinning yarns or just visiting with one another. Around the square and facing the courthouse on four sides were the retail stores, barber shops and small cafés. The courthouse was the stage, the locals with problems or with disagreements were the players and the employees and patrons of the surrounding businesses were the audience. This is where the action was and things could get hairy at times.

Hembree's Grocery was the best seat in the house— fifty-yard line and ground level. From the front of the store one could see the entire courthouse area and could pretty well keep abreast of all the happenings. The owner, Mr. Hembree, was a quiet and gentle man with a loyal cadre of employees and customers.

Once, while I was in the store, I noticed that employees and customers alike were drifting toward the front of the store and peering toward the courthouse. Obviously something was brewing on stage and the audience was gathering and riveted. Two big, tough-looking fellows were squared off at one another on the courthouse steps, in deep disagreement. One of the fellows, "Jake," was the local favorite, and the other was "that other fellow" that nobody seemed to know. Jake's fans were admonishing Jake to put that fellow's lights out, blow him away. One fan remarked that the "other fellow" must be a little bit dumb to challenge old Jake. Old Jake was obviously tough and well liked by the locals. However, as the next scene unveiled, "Old Jake" was flat on his back on the concrete and the "other fellow" was standing over him, bent over with both fists still knotted. Jake's fan club grew strangely quiet, the butcher went back to his meat market, the produce man went to the back and brought out some more turnip greens, the checkers went back to work and the customers resumed their shopping. Suddenly the audience was acting as though nothing had ever happened. Maybe another performance tomorrow?

Another story emanating from Hembree's Grocery

concerned the butcher, Adie. Adie was a huge man who spoke only when there was something to say. When he did speak, he was gruff and authoritative, and never changed expressions. Through the years, Adie grew on me and eventually became one of my most favorite people.

A new Baptist preacher had moved to town and was anxious to make his mark early. Adie was not a church-goer and when the new preacher found this out, one of his first objectives was to reach Adie somehow and get him to come to church. The young preacher decided to visit Adie down at the meat market in Hembree's Grocery, initiate a conversation with him and invite him to church on Sunday. The preacher walked into the store, smiling and greeting everyone as he worked his way back to Adie and the meat market. Adie was beginning to become suspicious, since the preacher didn't seem to be interested in buying any meat and was engaged in light conversation that didn't make any sense at all.

The preacher had a piece of mail in his hand, and out of frustration asked Adie where the post office was. Adie, without a word, pointed directly across the square to the post office. At this point, the preacher decided he had best deliver the message he came in to deliver in the first place.

"Adie, I want you to come to our church on Sunday, I just might be able to help you find Jesus."

Adie slowly and deliberately put his cleaver down on the chopping block, wiped his hands on his white apron, placed his huge elbows on top of the meat market and looked straight at the preacher. Then in gruff and measured tones, he said, "Preacher, if you can't so much as find the post office in Houston, Mississippi, how do you figure you can help me to find Jesus?"

View through the Open Door

Before there were motels in rural areas of Mississippi, there were scattered hotels in many of the small towns. The Ellard Hotel in Bruce was indeed unique. The first floor of this two-story structure housed the lobby, living quarters for the owner and the large dining room where guests could take their meals if they so chose. A rickety flight of stairs led up to a second floor hallway with rooms up and down each side, opening into the hallway. Mrs. Ellard, the owner, an elderly silver-haired lady, was simply too sweet and generous for her own good. All the bums for miles around had gotten the word that she was a soft touch and capitalized on it. On most any day at any meal there would be one or two obvious bums sitting at her corner table, filling their craws with Mrs. Ellard's good food. This sweet lady simply could not say "no" to anyone with a sad story.

One morning I checked into the hotel, carried my bags up to my room and went out into the surrounding area to work that day. On returning to my room that night it was obvious that someone had been in the room that day. The furniture was not as I had left it; my bag had been moved and the bed looked as though someone had been on it. My shaving brush and razor had been removed from my bag and were on the shelf in the bathroom. The brush still had suds on it. Of course I went downstairs and asked Mrs. Ellard if she could shed any light on these happenings. This sweet lady just dropped her head, gazed at the floor, wrung her hands in her apron and began to explain to me that this poor starving man came by that day and he also needed a bath and a shave. She began to explain to me that she knew I was a good man and wouldn't mind if she let him into my room.

"...Mrs. Ellard, do you know if he used my toothbrush?"

During another stay at the Ellard Hotel, I had another unique experience with a lady guest with whom I was sharing a bath. The bath was situated between our rooms with a door on each side leading to each room. When either of us used the bathroom, we simply hooked the latch on the door leading to the other guest's room. On leaving, we would unhook the door leading to the other room, exit the bathroom and close our door.

On this particular night I was sitting at a small desk, facing the door leading into the bathroom, when I heard my neighbor come into the bathroom, hook my door and proceed to run bathwater. Shortly I heard the water running out of the tub and the patter of bare feet on an old tile floor during the drying off process. Then I heard the sound of my door being unhooked. The old door had somehow come unfastened and when she unhooked it, it swung wide open, revealing the naked backside of a lady going back into her room. She never knew the door had opened.

I spotted the lady down at breakfast the next morning and was amazed at how nice she looked all dressed up. Without any clothes on, she seemed to be considerably more bottom-heavy.

Elmo and the Pussycat

For many years the husband and wife team of Elmo and Madge had done a superb job of building and managing their own grocery business. They were deeply devoted to each other in spite of the fact that their personality types were opposites. Madge, a sweet and caring lady, had a placid demeanor. Quietly intelligent, she was responsible for all the major business decisions in the store but made sure that her husband got all the credit. Elmo, on the other hand, was loud, gruff and pretentious. He wanted everyone to think he was the boss. He had a habit of loudly proclaiming "I tell it like it is." My experience had been that more often than not, rearing back and "telling it like it is" is an exercise in bad judgment. Elmo was brutally frank and proud of it. He just didn't have the smarts to understand that an end run or flanking maneuver is preferable to a frontal assault, be it as a military tactic or in person-to-person relationships. Without Madge to prop him up he would have fallen flat on his face. Many times I have seen him excuse himself when a decision had to be made and fake a trip to the bathroom in the back of the store. What he really wanted was to find Madge and get her input.

Elmo was consumed with hate. He hated taxes, the government, the president, the mayor and anyone else in authority. He was totally unimpressed by my suggestion to him that there is just so much room inside each of us and if we fill that room with hate, there is no space left for anything else. More than anything else, Elmo hated cats—pussycats, tomcats or little kittens. They were all the same to him. Madge, on the other hand, loved cats. When she spotted strays around the back of the store she couldn't resist feeding and cuddling them if possible. When Elmo would find that Madge had befriended a cat he would go berserk.

As I entered their store one day I spotted Madge

frantically signaling me to follow her to the back of the store, out of sight of Elmo. She was thoughtful enough to brief me before I went into the office to see Elmo and I was deeply grateful.

She explained to me that Elmo, on warm summer nights, had a habit of drawing his bath, getting into his pajamas and walking barefoot onto the back porch where he would yawn, stretch and "get a breath of fresh air," as he put it. On this particular night he had taken his bath, put on his pajamas and had walked barefoot out onto the back porch to go through his nightly routine. Unknown to him one of the neighbors had given Madge a potted plant in a stone pot and she had placed it on the edge of the back porch.

In the dim light that potted plant looked exactly like a squatting pussycat to Elmo. He figured Madge had been feeding another stray cat and he was furious. Right in the middle of his stretch he yelled "SCAT!"

Of course that stone pot didn't move. Elmo yelled even louder, "When I say 'SCAT,' by dang, I mean 'SCAT!'"

When that pot that looked like a squatting pussycat *still* didn't move Elmo strode into it like a field-goal kicker from fifty yards out and with all the strength he could muster he placed his bare right foot into what he thought was the soft underbelly of a pussycat. That stone pot was unforgiving. Elmo broke three toes and the bone in his foot.

When I went to the office to make my presentation to Elmo, I found him sitting in a tattered recliner with his right foot in a heavy cast and resting on a hassock. I broke a basic rule of good salesmanship when I didn't so much as mention his obvious infirmity. Neither did he.

Part II
Stories Laced with Fiction

First Date

Before grocery supermarkets came on the scene shoppers would most likely purchase their groceries from privately owned grocery stores. These were often family enterprises in which the husband, wife and all the kids worked. "Andy," an exceptional sixteen-year-old, was a part of one of these families. His father had been a customer of mine for many years and I had become very fond of Andy through those years. He and I would visit in the warehouse and he would pour out his soul to me. Andy seemed to like me. I think it was because I would listen to him. I had the feeling that no one else was listening.

One day as I entered the store I noticed that Andy seemed anxious to get me into the back of the store where we could talk. He was obviously uptight and dry-mouthed so I made myself immediately available. He told me about a cute little girl at school whom he liked very much and said that he was to have his first date with her that night. He was to walk her home from a school function. This time Andy wanted me to do more than listen—he wanted advice. Having no counseling skills, I tried to keep it simple. I told him I was sure that he knew right behavior—he had been taught by his family and had learned from having grown up as a churchgoer. All he had to do was be himself and show the young lady proper respect. Surprisingly our little session together seemed to settle him down.

As I pulled out onto the highway and headed to the next town I had a flashback to the night of my first date. Out in the country where we lived the center of our social activities was the Crossroads Baptist Church. There were no cars in the neighborhood so we all walked to the church services.

"Trudy" was the prettiest girl in the neighborhood and she came to all the church functions. Her mother was an excellent seamstress and made all of Trudy's cotton dresses, which seemed to reveal just enough of her full-figured body, but not too much. When Trudy would move around she would literally slither and slide underneath that cotton dress. She had a fair complexion and deep blue eyes that were half hidden by her flaming red hair. She had a charming little habit of flicking her head to her right and at the same time brushing her hair out of her face with her right hand. Then she would roll those big blue eyes at whoever she was talking to. When she rolled them at me, my knees would turn to jelly.

On what was to be my first date with Trudy, I asked if I could walk her home from church that night. She flicked her head to the right, brushed that red hair out of her face, rolled those blue eyes at me and half smiled as she said "Okay."

Suddenly I was dangerously weak-kneed. As we walked along that gravel road I told Trudy everything I knew about the weather and the crop prospects for that year. Then there we were on Weaver Creek bridge, looking down at the fragmented reflection of a pale moon in the trickle of water underneath. The creatures of the night were voicing their medley as an old owl called to his mate in the distance. This was just too much. I mustered the courage to reach over and take Trudy's hand. When she squeezed it, she unleashed a torrent of hormones that literally surged through my youthful body. We continued on toward her house and I was glad to get there, since I had exhausted all there was to say about the crops and the weather. We walked up to the doorsteps and I was preparing to shake hands with her and say goodnight when she suddenly turned to face me, put her arms around my neck, pressed her soft warm body close to mine and planted a kiss on me that curled my toes and crossed my eyes. After a period of heavenly bliss, Trudy unpeeled her body from mine, turned me loose and went inside her house. It was two miles home and I ran all the way. Hello, world!

The Mule Trader

"Donkey" McGee's store was situated on a very busy highway out on the edge of town. He had a thriving business, most of his customers being off the neighboring farms. At this time tractors and other mechanized farm equipment were indeed the exception on the surrounding farms. Farmers were instead proud of their mules. They would brag on their performance the same way some of us enjoy bragging about our cars today. Farmers would often get into heated arguments over the stamina or intelligence of one mule over another. Personally, I have never seen a stupid mule. They were always considerably smarter than we gave them credit for being.

I feel compelled at this point to digress for a moment to relate a story about my mule, old "Jack," that I plowed as a kid on the farm. "Jack" was a good partner for me—

he was slow but steady, smart but stubborn. When he would have a stubborn spell I would get frustrated and yank on the plow lines. Old Jack would raise his big white head and look around at me with his mouth wide open. So help me, that mule's profile reminded me of old Brother Gray, a Baptist preacher who preached down at the Crossroads Baptist Church every first Sunday. At this point I would feel guilty about the way I was treating old Jack and would let up on him. In retrospect, I am convinced old Jack was intelligent enough to know what was going on.

Unfortunately for old Jack, we discovered that he was a great mule to ride bareback. Riding old Jack when he hit his stride was comfortable as rocking in Grandma's front porch rocker. Consequently, we would plow him six days a week and ride him all day Sunday. Jack knew when Sunday came around and he would find himself a thicket to hide in. As smart as he was, he never seemed to figure out that when he raised his big white head over the thicket to see where we were, we could also see him.

Back to Donkey McGee. Behind his store he had a large barn and several acres of fenced pasture. At any time he had literally dozens of mules, some horses and a few billy goats. He was the classic mule trader—hence the name "Donkey."

Mule traders were a very special breed. To hear Donkey tell it he didn't have a mule over five years old. All of his mules were gentle, durable, smart and could plow all day on six ears of corn. If Donkey were in the used-car business today, he wouldn't have a car on his lot with over 35,000 miles on it. Every one would have been one-owner cars, owned by a little old lady who never drove it outside the city limits.

As I was leaving Donkey's store one day, he and I were standing by my car talking when an irate farmer came up leading a mule Donkey had sold him that morning. The farmer accused Donkey of knowingly selling him a blind mule. He claimed that when that old mule was hitched up, he just ambled around running into trees and fence posts. Donkey listened politely while the farmer said everything he had on his mind. (In the sales business, this is known as "letting him deflate his balloon.") Without a word in response, Donkey walked over to that mule, patted his head, looked into his mouth and then peered into his eyes, one at a time. He then turned, looked at the farmer and spoke slowly and deliberately, "That mule ain't blind—that mule just don't give a damn."

"Rooster Man" and the Clothesline

Miss Annie's country store was located on a gravel road about three miles out of town. She lived alone in living quarters connected to and behind her store. One of her bedrooms served as her warehouse, and checking her inventory meant crawling under the bed and going through the closet. Merchandise was stacked to the ceiling all around the room. She had no indoor plumbing, hence an "outhouse" back on the corner of her property. Miss Annie was a highly respected lady in the community and had a very good business.

"Rooster Man" was the Watkins Products salesman in the area. He canvassed the neighborhood on a regular basis, going house to house trying to sell his line of flavorings, spices and other goodies to the neighborhood women. On the back bumper of his old roadster he had securely fastened a chicken crate made of wire mesh stretched over a wood frame. In those days times were hard and money was short, and "Rooster Man" would accept most anything in trade for his products. That chicken crate always housed a mixture of chickens, ducks, geese and guineas as he made his rounds. He always seemed to have a crowing rooster—hence the name "Rooster Man."

Late one afternoon "Rooster Man" whipped his old roadster up into Miss Annie's parking lot, hurriedly jumped out and asked her if he could use her outhouse. It seems that "Rooster Man" had been bothered somewhat with constipation lately and the doctor had given him some medication to be taken when he got home that night. He decided to get a head start and took the medicine about an hour before heading home, but that turned out to be not overly smart. The urge hit him fast and hard just before he got to Miss Annie's store on his way home, and he knew that was as far as he could stretch it.

Of course, Miss Annie was happy for him to use her outhouse. "Rooster Man" knew that the shortest distance between two points is a straight line, so that's the route he took to that outhouse. Trouble was, Miss Annie had a tightly stretched clothesline, chin high, between him and the outhouse, and in the late afternoon dusk, with his bifocals, he never saw it. About the time he had gathered a full head of steam, that clothesline caught him right under the chin. He did a back flip and lay quietly on the ground under that clothesline. Miss Annie went running down to him, apologizing about her clothesline.

"Rooster Man" looked up at Miss Annie with a more

contented expression and said quietly, "Miss Annie, I don't think I could have made it anyway."

Bull Mountain Bottom Booze

Back in the days when bonded whiskey was illegal, the moonshiners of Bull Mountain Bottom made a name for themselves by producing a brew of unequaled zap. There were always stories circulating lending credibility to the potency of this particular moonshine. Nobody, it was said, who took a daily shot of the elixir would ever be bothered by having worms. One local imbiber was even said to have hair on his tongue. But none of the stories I had heard around Smithville compared to the one a customer in Amory told me one day as I called on him.

This customer's store faced on Main Street and the back of the store opened onto a large, open area between the backs of the stores and the railroad tracks. This open area, known as the Cotton Yard, was packed on weekends with farmers from miles around who had brought their produce into town to sell, trade or even give away. On Saturdays that Cotton Yard would be covered with farmers with chickens, pigs, calves, ducks, geese, guineas, mules, bales of hay and even bales of cotton. Might I add, I think it doubled as a social get-together for these good country folk who didn't have a great many opportunities to socialize otherwise.

One warm spring Saturday this customer told me he was standing in the back of his store, just enjoying the scene in the Cotton Yard. A crowd of mules, horses, wagons and farmers with all their goods was milling around as they sold, traded and gave away their wares. Scattered around the area, small circles of men were standing around laughing, talking, joking and just having great fun. One group was standing close enough to my customer's store that he could see and hear what was going on. One member of the group reached deep into his right rear overall pocket, pulled out a pint bottle, popped the corn cob stopper and they all began to sip at that bottle of Bull Mountain Bottom booze. A sip or two of that lightning at a time was all a man could handle, otherwise he would lose his breath for a spell. One of the group kept the bottle to his mouth too long and his cap flew off.

A vital part of this story has to do with a "tumble bug," known as a dung beetle in more polite circles. Unknown to these fellows, a tumble bug was moving around under their feet, looking for some dung to roll up into a ball, back up to, and roll away. However, that tumble bug's mission was to change drastically. These fellows spilled some of that lightning and three drops of it landed on top of that tumble bug. That bug just stood still for about three minutes while he absorbed that lightning. Then quick as a wink he took off. He circled that Cotton Yard twice before backing up to a bale of cotton and rolling it all the way to the loading ramp down by the railroad track.

"Pepper" Snell—Idea Man

The large corporation that I worked for and eventually retired from was constantly searching for young men with fresh new ideas. Time, itself, was a precious commodity and every minute of it on the job should be productive. In order to compete effectively in the marketplace, our company had to find better, faster and cheaper ways to get the job done, and bright young men with vision were brought on board each year to assure that this happened. Constantly heard at meetings and seminars was, "Don't work harder, work smarter."

Oftentimes when at meetings or seminars and the discussion turned to the need for new ideas and vision in our work, I would be reminded of an old character my dad used to tell me about who lived around the turn of the century. "Pepper" Snell was obviously a man of vision. Like da Vinci and Jules Verne, Pepper lived ahead of his time. He no doubt had a head full of new ideas and was a man of vision. When he looked at the forest he didn't just see the trees along the edge, he saw all the way over in the woods. The trouble was that in those days in the rural hill country of Mississippi there was no radio, no television or other means of communication. Consequently Pepper's visions and his ideas were confined to the community in which he lived. He had supposedly built a clothesline for his wife that was mounted on rollers fastened to the house near a kitchen window and to a hackberry tree in the backyard. His wife could hang the wash right out her kitchen window, never having to go outside. Of course she could bring in the dry clothes in the same manner. Pepper had an arrangement of mirrors all around his house that reflected somehow into a larger mirror just outside his kitchen window. He claimed he could look out the window into the larger mirror and see all around his house.

Pepper at some point in his life became consumed

with the principle of human flight. He would sit for long periods of time watching the vultures and hawks as they sailed effortlessly and the other smaller birds as they flapped their wings and moved among the trees. He was convinced that man could fly if he could construct himself a proper set of wings and he wasn't at all shy about propounding his theory. He was sharply criticized by the locals who were equally convinced that if God had intended man to fly he would have provided him with those wings. Pepper's response to that was that God gave him a brain and expected him to use it.

Pepper devoted all his talents over the next few weeks to the construction of a suitable pair of wings that would enable him to fly. He had reworked two large umbrellas with straps that could be tightly fastened to his arms. Pepper was a good PR man too—he made sure every one in the community knew what he was doing and notified them of the day he planned to make his first flight.

On the appointed day the crowds began to gather. Whole families arrived in horse-drawn wagons; some had walked for miles and others came on horseback. When everyone had gathered, Pepper announced to the crowd that he would launch his flight from the highest point of the barn roof. The crowd moved to the front of the barn. Pepper's wife helped him to tightly strap on his wings and he climbed a rickety ladder to the roof. His adrenaline was flowing as he made his way to the highest part of the roof and looked down at the crowd. Pepper stretched up on his toes and spread his wings. The crowd below gasped and sighed.

Pepper's wife looked up at her husband, cupped her hands to her mouth and yelled in a shrill voice that all could hear, "Pa, you fly around close, now, so we can all see you!"

Shortly thereafter he spread his wings and launched, flapping his wings as he plummeted to the ground below. Fortunately the muck and mire in front of the barn cushioned his fall sufficiently that Pepper survived to give birth to other new ideas. Who knows what contribution Pepper could have made had he lived in our world of today.

Fresh Meat for "Blue"

Grocery store butchers in the old days were usually big, bald, jolly and strong. They had to be strong if they were to muscle a quarter of beef out of the cooler over to the cutting table. "Big Al" Dobbs fit the mold. He was over six feet tall, red-faced, and bald. And he talked without ceasing. Just keeping his 285 pounds upright and moving around was labor enough to bring out little clear beads of perspiration on his big forehead even in January.

In those days Saturday night country dances were the place to go. A country band usually consisted of a fiddle, twin guitars, a banjo and a mandolin. The band always wanted a little money for playing and the first order of business was to pass the hat around. Times were hard, money was short and the band wasn't always pleased with the offering. The band would handle that by tuning up, playing just enough of a dance tune to get the dancers going and then abruptly stop. The band's spokesman, the fiddler, would put his fiddle across his knees, fold his arms and explain that the offering wasn't even enough to buy a set of strings. If they wanted to dance, they would have to pay the fiddler. After passing the hat another time or two the band would resume playing and the house would start to rock to the beat of the two-step.

"Big Al" loved to dance and never missed one of these Saturday night affairs. He and his girlfriend, Maybelle, were the center of attention once they got warmed up.

On this particular Saturday night a farmer in the community, Ben Hall, was hosting the affair. As the folks began to gather, Ben's old blue tick hound, "Blue," became restless. His bed consisted of two feed sacks on the south side of a stack of firewood on the front porch. None of the crowd coming across the front porch so much as gave Blue a glance, but Blue became increasingly nervous as the crowd gathered. He had pressed in as close as possible to that stack of firewood and was huddled quietly.

The crowd gathered, the music started and that old house began to rock. Big Al and Maybelle were putting on a show. Eventually all the other dancers moved over to the side and gave center stage to Big Al and Maybelle. The trouble was that Big Al got a bit too excited and stomped his left heel down a bit too hard on the "one" count of the two-step. That piece of one-by-twelve pine flooring broke and Big Al's left foot and leg plunged through all the way to the ground. The crowd was delighted until they noticed Big Al was crying out with pain and couldn't move from the spot.

With Maybelle's help he began to slowly pull his leg up out of that hole in the floor and when he did he pulled that hound dog's head up also. Old Blue had sunk his teeth into Big Al's leg just above the ankle and was reluctant to turn loose. Apparently all that bedlam in the house had gotten old Blue so upset that he had left his bed on the porch and had taken refuge under the house. Maybelle finally kicked the dog loose from Big Al's leg and helped Big Al into the kitchen. Maybelle sat him down in a straight chair, pulled up his pants leg and placed his foot on top of that oilcloth covered kitchen table. She then washed the bleeding wound with kerosene and wrapped it tightly with strips of cloth torn from an old bed sheet. A few minutes later both of them were back on the floor with the other dancers. As they "two-stepped" around that hole in the middle of the floor Big Al was noticeably more cautious. Now and then old Blue would poke his head up through that hole in the floor and check things out—or maybe he was looking for some more fresh meat.

Deacon Dexter

Grocery shopping in the rural south in the 1940s and 1950s was not a matter of choosing between a Kroger, Winn-Dixie, or Albertson's. It was rather a matter of choosing between any one of several family-owned grocery stores in the area. Dexter's Grocery was one such store. It had been owned and operated by the Dexter family for generations and was now managed by a son of the current owners, Delbert Dexter.

Delbert was a good and honorable man though not at all impressive physically. Tall, thin and slightly stooped, his seemingly too long arms dangled loosely from his shoulders as he walked the aisles of the store trying to keep his employees busy at whatever task they were assigned. Mostly the younger employees ignored him. Delbert's easy manner was by no means conducive to getting the best effort from these youngsters. When his back was turned they would mock him and make fun of him. Nevertheless, these youngsters knew deep down that Delbert Dexter was a fair man, and when the chips were down, they were loyal to him.

Delbert was a faithful member of Mt. Prospect Baptist Church. He was at the church for every service and made himself readily available to serve in any capacity. At night and on Sunday afternoons Delbert's old Buick could be seen all over the area as he visited the sick and ministered to shut-ins. The older people in the area always referred to him affectionately as "Deacon Dexter."

In those days a felt hat was a necessary part of a man's Sunday attire. The churches had hat racks and tables in the rear where the men could place their hats when entering the church. On a typical Sunday the hat racks would be full and the table covered with men's hats. When the pastor would ask the ushers to come forward for a prayer before taking the offering, each would get his hat and carry it down to the altar to be used as a collection plate.

Deacon Dexter always helped to take up the collection but the pastor never asked him to lead the prayer. He and the others present knew that this good man, Deacon Dexter, simply could not pray in public. As Delbert himself put it, "When I stand up, my mind sits down."

A new pastor came to serve at Mt. Prospect and when he learned of Deacon Dexter's dilemma he was determined to counsel the poor man through his problem. The Pastor began by suggesting to Delbert that he write a short prayer on a piece of paper and stick it down in the top of his hat. Then when he brought his hat down for the prayer before taking the offering, he could simply read the prayer as he stood with head bowed. Delbert agreed to give it a try and wrote out a prayer on a piece of paper that would fit down inside his hat.

Sunday morning came around and Deacon Dexter was ready to give the people in the congregation the surprise of their lives. The pastor asked the ushers to come forward and they all walked down to the altar with their hats in their hands. The good deacon was extremely nervous but excited and confident.

As the ushers stood in front of the altar the pastor did the unthinkable and asked Deacon Dexter to lead the prayer. A dead hush fell over the congregation as Delbert held his hat in front of him, squinted down into it through half-closed eyes, and said, "Dear Father..." Then he paused and you could have heard a pin drop in that Baptist church. After a moment of deathly silence, a panic-stricken Deacon Dexter blurted out frantically and loud enough for all to hear, "Oh God! This ain't my hat!"

And Then There Was One

Freddie had for many years been manager of a grocery business owned by a well-to-do family in this small hill country town. In my many years of selling to men in the grocery industry I had called on literally hundreds of buyers, but not one came close to Freddie in gentlemanly makeup. He was quiet, caring, polite and always ready to listen to what a sales representative had to say. Even if his answer was "No," you would still go away feeling good inside about some little something he had said or done. Freddie's gentle demeanor was the exception rather than the rule in a tough business. What a fortunate woman his wife was to have a husband like Freddie.

One day after calling on Freddie I walked across the street to Joe's Diner for a cup of the best coffee in the area. Joe's little café up front was just a cover for the illicit activities being conducted in a pool room in back. That pool room was headquarters for bootlegging and gambling in the area. Joe even had some girls that always hung around. If drugs had been available in those days, that pool room would have been the marketplace.

I walked in, took a seat at the counter and asked Joe to draw me a hot cup out of the bottom of the pot. There was nobody up front but I could hear the clacking of pool balls in back. Joe pushed the steaming mug across the counter and sat down on a stool opposite me. He propped his elbows on the counter, rested his biscuit-shaped face in his cupped hands and we began to visit. When I mentioned what pure pleasure it was to call on Freddie and what a complete gentleman he seemed to be, old Joe clapped his greasy hands over his head and very nearly fell off that stool as he guffawed hilariously. After regaining his composure he began to tell me how it used to be with Freddie. It was difficult for me to believe such a Dr. Jekyll and Mr. Hyde story about Freddie, but I lingered through three refills and listened intently as Joe told his story.

According to Joe, Freddie and his wife moved to town many years ago and settled in a small bungalow about a quarter of a mile out of town. Freddie worked six days a week and always got paid at the end of the day on Saturday. Every Saturday after getting paid he would drop by Joe's place for just one drink before walking home. Whiskey does different things to different people. In

Freddie's case it threw a 180-degree change on his personality. After the first drink he had to have another and another. After about the third drink he would convince himself that he was God's gift to women and the girls that hung around would take advantage of him. Eventually he would stagger home along that gravel road to a wife who would be wringing her hands, weeping and begging him to change his ways. After sobering up he would be truly repentant.

Then one Saturday night events transpired in Freddie's life that would change him completely. On this particular week-end his wife's mother, father and sister were visiting. Freddie got his pay envelope as usual and was determined to head home after that one drink. However, he lost control and it was not to be. After lingering much too long in that den of iniquity he staggered out the door and started down that gravel road home. It was a clear night and a full moon was shining so brightly that it appeared to be the sole occupant of the night sky. As he stumbled along, the loose gravel crunching under his feet, he agonized over how he was going to handle the situation when he arrived home.

Suddenly, in a ditch, he saw a dead cow that had been hit by a vehicle earlier that night. The answer came to him.

He got down in that ditch, took his Barlow knife and cut out the part of the cow's bag that had the four teats on it. He stuck that cow's bag down in the front of his pants, continued to his house and walked up on the porch. His wife turned on the porch light and met him on the porch as she wrung her hands and cried. Freddie confronted her on unsteady feet, and mumbled that he was going to take care of his problem once and for all. At this point he unzipped his pants, pulled out one of those teats, cut it off with his knife and pitched it under a rose bush at the end of the porch. His wife piled up in a dead faint.

His mother-in-law met him in the living room with her arms folded tightly across her chest, slowly shaking her head from side to side. Freddie told her the same thing as he unzipped his pants again, pulled out the second teat, cut it off and threw it in the corner. She, too, fainted.

In the den the father-in-law was sprawled in Freddie's favorite chair, permeating the air in the area as he puffed on his corncob pipe packed with Sir Walter Raleigh pipe tobacco. The old man gave Freddie a disapproving look. Freddie responded by telling him the same thing he had told the others. Then he unzipped his pants again, pulled out the third teat, cut it off and threw it in a wastebasket. The old fellow slid down in his chair as though asleep, his pipe dangling loosely from the corner of his mouth.

In the kitchen Freddie found his sister-in-law stirring a pot on the stove. Before she could voice a complaint Freddie told her the same thing as he unzipped his pants, pulled out the fourth teat, cut it off and pitched it into a waste can. She fainted. Quite pleased with himself, Freddie staggered out the back porch, reached down into his pants and removed that cow's bag. As he was placing it in the garbage can, he noticed it still had one teat left on it. That's when Freddie fainted.

Part III

Stories in a Serious Vein

One Good Man

During my thirty-three and one half years of traveling the highways and byways of rural Mississippi, calling on both wholesalers and retailers in the grocery business, my path cross the paths of hundreds of wonderful people. Some few were of such sterling character that they remain fresh in my memory even now. Just such a man was "Mr. Ed."

Before chain store supermarkets came on the scene, small grocery stores and meat markets were scattered around the neighborhoods serving customers in the area. Most would deliver groceries to customers and all would serve on credit. Customers would pay their bills weekly or monthly. Store owners would have to be selective with credit customers, since there was no collateral to repossess in the case of non-payment. Of course there were always some deadbeat credit customers who would pay their bills for a few weeks or months, run up a big bill, and then simply disappear. Savvy store owners would usually know who these deadbeats were and would protect themselves against them by tacking extra charges on to their bills each pay period. Hopefully by the time the deadbeat had decided to skip out, the owner would already have his money.

Mr. Ed had held a good job with a local industry for many years and had apparently accumulated considerable savings. As he told me later, he had always had a desire to own a neighborhood grocery store. Past middle age, he quit his job, took his life savings, borrowed some additional funds and purchased a building, fixtures and inventory. The first month or two he was the happiest he had ever been.

Mr. Ed was a giant of a man. Everything to him was funny and when he laughed, his huge stomach would bounce up and down. I remember sitting in his little office opposite him in his oversized chair as he leaned his massive upper torso over on his little desk that creaked under the load.

As I continued to call on Mr. Ed, his sterling qualities of character began to shine through. Inside that barreled chest beat a big warm heart, filled with caring and compassion. He was too good to the deadbeat credit customers and they were taking advantage of him. As time passed, his inventory began to grow thin, a sure sign that his suppliers were becoming concerned about his credit worthiness. In spite of this he never lost his happy outlook or his readiness to laugh.

On my last call on this good man who was obviously in financial trouble, he and I sat in his tiny office. I suggested to him that maybe he should do as some of my other customers have done—tack an extra amount on these questionable credit consumers' bills every month. Then if they left him, he already had their money. This no doubt struck a responsive chord. He cocked his head to one side thoughtfully and focused his eyes on a small spider that was busily spinning a web up in the northeast corner of his office. He pondered my suggestion for a moment before dropping his head and turning toward me with a wry smile on his face. Then he said quite simply, "Mr. Carter, that wouldn't be right."

My guess is that as he pondered my suggestion and

watched that little spider weave its web he took a trip back in time to his early childhood when a good and loving mother instilled in him the necessity of doing that which is right without regard for the consequences. He then reached into his desk, pulled out a letter with a Chicago postmark and began to read it to me as he chuckled. "Dear Mr. Ed. This letter is to let you know that I am going to pay you what I owe you." Then came the clincher. "But not now."

On my next trip to the area Mr. Ed's store was padlocked and he was in bankruptcy. A few days later the big warm heart of Mr. Ed quit beating. He died suddenly of a heart attack. St. Peter must have needed an addition to his team—right away.

A Wasted Mind

Sonny's Supermarket was located in a small town in rural Mississippi and served the surrounding farm community. The business was successfully run by Sonny, his wife and children. The children grew up working in the store and at one time or another each of them had handled every responsibility in the business. The considerable volume of business done by the store made it necessary for Sonny to maintain a sizable warehouse adjacent to the main building. Nowhere in my territory was there a warehouse as well organized as this one. All merchandise was neatly stacked according to brands and sizes, with adequate aisle space providing easy immediate access to any piece of inventory that might be needed up front. Inventory control was as good as I had ever seen. This well run warehouse was the responsibility of and existed because of one very exceptional person, an elderly black man—"Nap" Tatum.

Nap was a quiet man of obvious intelligence and perception. As the years passed and Nap and I grew to be friends, we would sit in that warehouse and share philosophies, personal anecdotes and opinions on world problems. The depth and clarity of his thinking never ceased to amaze me.

One day in my presence he was admonishing two of the owner's boys that had been into mischief of some kind. Of course they ignored him. Nap's response, "There ain't no waste of time like that spent trying to introduce wisdom to a d__d fool." These words could have easily come from Emerson. Surely this man must have formal education beyond high school. I had never asked him, and he had never mentioned it.

Things were quiet on this particular day in the warehouse, so Nap and I sat down alongside each other on a couple of sacks of mule feed and began to visit. Nap seemed to be in a somber and reflective mood. As he began to tell me things I already knew about him—how he kept inventory under control, kept all brands and sizes properly stored and how he could give the owner movement figures on any brand or size, it became obvious to me that he was leading up to much bigger things that I *didn't* know about.

I sat quietly and listened but watched him out of the corner of my eye. His face became painfully drawn as he prepared to deliver the message that I was to hear today. Suddenly and forcefully he spoke these words, "I can't read one word or write one word. I have never been to school a day in my life. I handle this inventory by memorizing the designs on the boxes and sacks." Nap lighted up somewhat as though a load was lifted from his shoulders. I remained quiet in my shock and near disbelief.

Nap then began to relate to me the story of his childhood. He was one of six children who grew up on his father's farm in the area. Adjacent to the farm was a one-room school where the black kids in the area could learn to read, write, add and subtract. However, Nap's father was a hard working man who thought attending school was a waste of time . . . what a young boy needed to do was learn to work. Then he could make a living.

Nap, at an early age, must have recognized that he had enormous capability and talent. He must have had a gnawing hunger for knowledge. On days when the weather was such that he knew the school windows would be open, he would slip over to the school and huddle outside an open window, listening to every word the teacher spoke, hoping to learn to read. When his dad would catch him at the little school he would give him a thrashing that hurt for a week. However, Nap's yearning for knowledge was so intense that he would continue to slip over to that little school.

Nap became silent. I continued to watch him out of the corner of my eye. He slowly leaned forward and placed his elbows on his knees. As he rested his chin in his cupped hands his eyes seemed to be fixed on the long ago and the far away as he dwelt on what could have been . . . what should have been . . . but never was. A big fat tear rolled down his left cheek and splattered in the dust on the warehouse floor. Unashamedly, I joined him.

Wisdom of the Years

Mr. Shack dropped out of high school and began working in a wholesale grocery business in order to help support his family during the Great Depression. He began as an errand boy and floor sweeper but very soon began to move up to levels of more and more responsibility. He worked hard, he was dependable and he was honest. After several years he had worked his way up to the position of manager, and at this time, some thirty years later, he had bought the business. He had graduated from the "school of hard knocks" and deserved a degree with honors. Now he sat behind a big desk in a big office and had his own secretary and sales force.

On my first few calls on this good man it became evident that he harbored some resentment toward me, a university graduate and somewhat cocky youngster, telling him, a high school dropout, what to do. On a previous call I had tried to get him to buy into a promotion which I was sure would be beneficial to him, but he refused. As it happened, the promotion was a hot one and he missed out on it. Now I was trying to tell him how he could have profited if he had done as I had asked him. Suddenly he pounded the top of his desk with a stubby fist, looked me cold in the eye and began to deliver to me the first of two bits of wisdom I was going to receive that day. He held me spellbound as he explained to me in rather emphatic terms that we move forward from where we *are*, not from where we would have been *if*. He went on to say that spending too much time looking back at what we *should* have done is a bit like driving down a busy highway and spending too much time looking into the rear-view mirror. Sooner or later we will find ourselves wedged under the rear end of an eighteen-wheeler. Mr. Shack was on a roll and I was shortly to hear the second bit of wisdom for the day. For some reason my presentation did not go well with him. Something in the manner of my speech, or possibly some ill-chosen words on my part led him to once again pound that desk top and accuse me of thinking I was a pretty smart dude. He arose from his desk, walked around by my side, took me by the arm and escorted me over to a window that looked down on a busy street below. It was getting late in the day and pedestrians of every walk of life were scurrying along in every direction. A little old lady was walking a dog. A nattily dressed gentleman had a brief-case tight under his arm. A laborer in greasy coveralls checked his watch as he hurried along. Certainly a cross-section of the local population was represented in the passing parade. I was consumed with curiosity as we both quietly watched the scene on the street. Then Mr. Shack slowly turned to face me and in father-to-son tone delivered to me the second bit of wisdom I was to receive on this day. "Son, I know you think you are pretty smart, but remember this—any one of those characters on the street down there can tell you *something* you don't know."

After all these years the memory of Mr. Shack is very much alive. A high school dropout, he was a special friend and mentor to me, and a master teacher in the art of living. He taught me things about life that I somehow or other missed in four years at the university and in the days at seminars.

Seriously, Now

I worked for many years and eventually retired from one

of the country's large corporations, doing business in all fifty states and in what was at that time known as the free world. Company headquarters was, and still is, in Cincinnati. Once when I was in our headquarters building in Cincinnati with some time to kill, I was approached in the lobby by a young company employee who was permanently stationed there. He asked me if I would like to see the eleventh floor. We all knew that the eleventh floor was the top floor of the building and that it housed the offices of the top management people of the company. It was serviced by a special elevator and only people with very good reason used it—and then only under escort. Of course I wanted to see the eleventh floor.

On the way up the elevator, the young man explained to me that when we stepped off the elevator and as we walked the hallway we would speak only in whispers. This particular floor of the building was so completely insulated from outside noises that sound from the streets below could not be heard—no honking of horns, no sirens, no sounds of eighteen-wheelers changing gears. An eerie quiet prevailed on the eleventh floor.

As we moved around the hallway, the young man pointed out to me the offices of top management people, all very familiar names. We rounded a corner and he pushed open a large heavy door and we stepped through it into a cavernous room. One end of the room was covered by a giant projection screen and to one side was a booth containing electronic devices that I didn't understand. A large, oval, highly-polished mahogany table occupied the middle of the room with chairs on each side and one chair at each end. I recognized this as the Board of Directors meeting room and was impressed as he told me the names of men of stature in the business world who sat in each chair on each side of the table. At the head of the table sat the Chairman of the Board, explained the young man, but he failed to mention who sat in the chair at the other end. I asked the obvious question. His answer was that the chair in question was an extra one—that it represented the stockholders of the company. He further remarked that when the Board was around this table and in session, you could be sure that they now and then glanced at that extra chair, saw seated in it the stockholders of the company, the ones in the final analysis they were responsible to, and handled their business accordingly.

Suddenly it struck me that big business and my church back home were structured in similar fashion. My church also had boards, committees and commissions. Each one had its chairman. Certainly the church is also big business—it's God's business, the biggest business there is around.

At this particular time my church back home was planning its agenda for the coming year. The various committees were holding meetings to figure their budgets and set their objectives for the immediate future.

The thought came to me that those of us in the church who are charged with the responsibility of serving on committees and with making decisions that determine the direction the church will move during the next year could learn something from corporate America. Maybe it would be a good thing for us when we meet, like big business, to pull up that extra chair, but see seated in it a man named Jesus, the one in the final analysis *we* are responsible to, and handle our business accordingly.